LESSONS IN LOVE

fLiRT

Also available in the series:

Never Too Late

fLiRT

LESSONS IN LOVE

A. DESTINY & CATHERINE HAPKA

SIMON PULSE

NEW YORK   LONDON   TORONTO   SYDNEY   NEW DELHI

SIMON PULSE

An imprint of Simon & Schuster Children's Publishing Division

1230 Avenue of the Americas, New York, NY 10020

First Simon Pulse edition February 2014

Text copyright © 2014 by Simon & Schuster, Inc.

Cover photograph copyright © 2014 by Paul Bradbury/Getty Images

All rights reserved, including the right of reproduction in whole or in part in any form.

SIMON PULSE and colophon are registered trademarks of Simon & Schuster, Inc.

For information about special discounts for bulk purchases, please contact Simon & Schuster Special Sales at 1-866-506-1949 or business@simonandschuster.com.

The Simon & Schuster Speakers Bureau can bring authors to your live event. For more information or to book an event contact the Simon & Schuster Speakers Bureau at 1-866-248-3049 or visit our website at www.simonspeakers.com.

Designed by Regina Flath

The text of this book was set in Adobe Caslon Pro.

Manufactured in the United States of America

10 9 8 7 6 5 4 3 2 1

Library of Congress Cataloging-in-Publication Data:

Destiny, A.

Flirt : lessons in love / by A. Destiny & Catherine Hapka. —

First Simon Pulse paperback edition.

p. cm.

Summary: Fifteen-year-old, science loving Bailey experiences what it is like to fall in love for the first time when new boy Logan Morse arrives into town.

[1. Dating (Social customs)—Fiction. 2. High schools—Fiction. 3. Schools—Fiction. 4. Friendship—Fiction. 5. Restaurants—Fiction.] I. Hapka, Catherine. II. Title.

PZ7.D475Fli 2014

[Fic]—dc23

2013029380

ISBN 978-1-4424-8401-6 (hc)

ISBN 978-1-4424-8400-9 (pbk)

ISBN 978-1-4424-8402-3 (eBook)

Chapter ● One

It started as just another normal Sunday afternoon. I was wiping down tables at College Avenue Eats. That was normal. My family had owned the place for three generations, and I worked there part-time after school and on weekends.

We were between the end of brunch and the start of the dinner rush, so the place was pretty quiet. There were a couple of university students at the little round tables by the big front window, heads bent over their laptops. An old guy at the counter was nursing a cup of coffee and reading the local paper. Still normal.

My best friend, Simone Amrou, was in the corner booth cramming for tomorrow's biology test. *Definitely* normal. "Opposites attract" was a perfectly sound scientific principle (magnetism, anyone?), but even if it wasn't, I would have believed it based on my lifelong friendship with Simone.

Exhibit A? I'd started studying for the test the same day Mr. Ba announced it two weeks earlier. Simone? Not so much.

"Help me, Bailey!" she wailed as I straightened the salt and pepper shakers on the next table. She widened her puppy-dog brown eyes and stared at me soulfully. That generally worked on guys, especially paired with her exotic good looks. On me? Nuh-uh.

"I told you to read the chapters as we went along." I flicked a stray cupcake crumb off a chair with my rag. "Then you wouldn't have to cram at the last minute."

"I know, Miss Logic, I know." Simone sighed, poufing out her already-full lips to blow a strand of wavy dark hair out of her face. "But I was busy with that English paper all last week, and then Matt wanted to hang out at the park yesterday—"

"Bailey!"

This time it was my cousin calling me from behind the counter. Susannah was nineteen, four years older than me, and a sophomore at the university.

"Be right back," I told Simone. When I reached the counter, Susannah was staring at the cash register with a peevish expression on her round, pretty face. "What's wrong?" I asked. "Did Methuselah die again?"

That was what we called the ancient cash register, which had been around since my great-grandparents started the business. My family was nothing if not consistent.

"Not this time, thank goodness." Susannah smiled, making deep dimples appear on both cheeks. "Do you know where your mom put the register tapes? I can't find them, and she just left to pick up your sister at gymnastics. I can call her, but you know she never picks up when she's driving, and—"

"No, it's okay. I'll find them." I hurried through the swinging saloon-style doors leading into the kitchen. My dad and Uncle Rick—Susannah's father—were just coming in from the delivery bay out back, both of them lugging tubs of donut glaze.

"Can you get the door, Bailey?" Dad grunted as he hoisted his tubs onto the big marble-topped island where Mom and Great-Aunt Ellen rolled out the pastry for the bakery business and the bread for the deli stuff.

I kicked the door shut, then grabbed one of the tubs my uncle was juggling and set it on the stainless-steel counter along the wall. "Suz can't find the register tapes," I said. "Has Mom been reorganizing again?"

My dad traded an amused look with Uncle Rick, who was Mom's brother. "Always," Dad said. "Check the blue cabinet. I think she put the office supplies in there this time."

"Thanks." I headed for the supply room. Everyone in the family knew Mom loved to reorganize. The problem was, she usually moved everything around and then forgot to tell anyone else where she put it all.

When I passed through the kitchen again, Dad was stowing

the last of the tubs under the counter, and Uncle Rick was on the phone.

"Three dozen mixed sandwiches for a week from Saturday?" He jotted something on a pad. "Got it. Will that be delivery or pickup?"

"Spring Thing order?" I asked Dad quietly. The Spring Thing was an annual event at the university—three days of fun, special events, and goofiness to celebrate spring before the crunch of finals set in.

"Guess so." He rubbed his bald spot the way he always did when he was distracted. "Can't believe how many orders we've got already. Gonna be a busy weekend."

"That's good, right? The more orders we get, the more money we make."

He grinned and tousled my chin-length brown hair as if I were still eight years old. "That's my girl," he said. "Always the math whiz!"

"Funny." I smacked his hand away with a laugh, then headed out front with the register tape.

Susannah was on a stool behind the deli case, hunched over a thick textbook. The page it was open to had tons of tiny text and no pictures at all.

"Got a test coming up?" I asked.

"Always." Susannah wrinkled her nose and glared at the book. "Tell me again why I decided to major in business administration? This stuff just doesn't make any sense!"

The little brass bell over the door jingled. A man I vaguely recognized as one of the English professors at the university came in.

Susannah watched as the professor paused to scan the specials board. "Is Deena back from break yet?" she asked me. "Looks like I'm about to have a sandwich order. And the evening crowd will start trickling in pretty soon."

"Don't think so, but our dads are both back there." I flipped open Methuselah's case, which gave way with a creak, and quickly changed out the tape. "They can make a sandwich if they have to."

As Susannah greeted the customer, I headed over to see how Simone was doing. She grabbed my arm and dragged me down onto the seat beside her. "You have to help me, Bails!" She sounded desperate. "I'm so going to flunk tomorrow!"

I glanced at the table. Her textbook was covered in Post-it notes, and other random bits of paper were scattered everywhere. "Okay, where are you stuck?"

"Everywhere," she moaned. "Starting with, what's the difference between DNA and RNA again?"

I sighed. Sadly, this too was normal.

"Okay, so they're both nucleic acids, right?" I said.

She looked blank. "Right?"

"Simone! Didn't you do *any* of the reading?" This was bad even for her. Mr. Ba's class was tough, and he didn't tolerate slackers. It was an accelerated class, and he expected his students to be serious about learning. I loved that. It made me feel like I was already in college learning real stuff instead of marking time in high school.

"I *read* it." Simone stuck her lower lip out in that cute little pout that drove boys crazy. "I just didn't *understand* it. We can't all be science geniuses like you, Myers."

The bell jingled again as another customer came in. I glanced over automatically. I didn't recognize him, which definitely *wasn't* normal, since he was a guy about my own age. There was only one high school in our town, and it was small enough for everyone to know everyone else, by face if not necessarily by name.

Simone spotted the new arrival too. "Who's *that*?" she hissed, elbowing me hard in the ribs.

"Ow! I don't know." I rubbed my ribs and sneaked another look at the guy. He was in line behind the professor, checking out the stuff in the bakery display case while he waited. Kind of tall. Dark brown hair that curled at the temples and the back of his neck. A nose that was a little long and slopey in a way that made his whole face more interesting.

"Maybe he goes to that Catholic school out by the mall," Simone whispered. "Oh! Or he could be a senior from out of town who's touring the campus."

"He doesn't look old enough to be a senior." I shot her a sly look. "But it's a good thing if he's from out of town. You're going out with Matt now, remember? And this guy looks like just the type to tempt you—you know, tall, dark, and handsome."

She tore her gaze away from the guy just long enough to raise one perfectly groomed eyebrow at me. "Yeah, he is pretty cute. It's not like *you* to notice that, though, Bails."

"What? I have eyes." I quickly busied myself straightening her mess of papers. "So back to DNA versus RNA . . ."

"That can wait. Come on, let's go say hi." Simone shoved me out of the booth so energetically I almost hit the floor. I recovered with a less-than-graceful lurch and a grab at the nearest table. Tossing a look toward the counter, I was relieved to see that the guy had his back to me.

"Wait," I hissed. "What are you going to say to him?"

Simone ignored me, grabbing my hand and dragging me along. With my free hand, I quickly smoothed down my hair as best I could. How much had Dad messed it up just now?

And more to the point, what difference did it make? As soon as Mr. Tall Dark and Handsome got a look at Simone, he wouldn't spare a glance for my hair if it was on fire. That was life, and I was used to it. Kind of liked it, actually—it saved me from a lot of embarrassment and stress. Because while I had no trouble chatting with other girls or adults, I was notoriously tongue-tied around guys my own age. I just never seemed to know what to say when faced with that Y chromosome. I was pretty sure it was some kind of syndrome. Maybe I could do a study on it after med school.

Simone, however, was not similarly afflicted. "Hi, there!" she said brightly, tapping the guy on the shoulder. "I'm Simone, and this is my friend Bailey. Are you new in town?"

The guy looked startled, but then he smiled. "Is it that obvious?"

Simone let out her giddiest, most charming laugh. "Only because this is, like, the smallest town in the universe. Right, Bails?"

"Uh?" I said. "I mean, yeah. Except for the university. If you include the student body, I mean, it's actually quite . . . But that's not, you know . . ."

Okay, yes, I was floundering. Obviously. Luckily, Simone came to the rescue. "So are you here for a campus tour, or what?" she asked the guy.

"Not exactly." He looked even cuter when he smiled. "My family just moved here. Actually, we're in the middle of moving in right now—that's why my parents sent me out to pick up some food." He gestured vaguely at the deli counter. "Our new kitchen's kind of a mess."

"You came to the right place," Simone told him. "Eats has the best food in town—just ask Bailey. Her family has run it for like the past million years."

"Really? Cool." The guy turned and studied my face. His eyes were very blue. I held my breath. What was I supposed to do now? My mind was a vacuum. Not as in vacuum cleaner. As in the scientific term for a complete absence of matter or substance.

This time it was Susannah who came to my rescue. "Can I help you?" she called out as the professor moved out of the way, clutching a steaming cup of coffee.

"Yeah, thanks." Mr. Blue Eyes stepped forward. "I need to order some sandwiches to go. . . ."

As he started to give his order, I yanked Simone away. "We should get back to studying."

"Are you mental? We can't abandon your hot new friend." She poked me in the side, making me squawk. "Didn't you see how he was looking at you? And he's obviously smart, too. Just your type."

"What? No. What do you—shut up." I frowned at her.

The loud *cha-ching!* of Methuselah's cash drawer distracted me. I glanced over just as Susannah said "Okay, that'll be about five, ten minutes."

"Thanks." The guy barely had time to turn and face us again before Simone reached out and tugged lightly on the sleeve of his T-shirt.

"MIT, huh?" she said. "That just happens to be Bailey's dream school."

I blinked, noticing his shirt for the first time. It was gray with the red MIT logo emblazoned across the chest. How had I missed that? Or wait—had my subconscious mind somehow picked up on it without telling the rest of me? Maybe that explained why my attention was drawn to this guy with the strength of a neodymium magnet.

"Yeah, both my parents went there," the guy said. "By the way, I'm Logan. Logan Morse."

"Like Morse code?" I blurted out.

See? Hopeless at talking to guys.

Logan laughed. "No relation, as far as I know."

"So Logan," Simone said. "Why'd your family move here?"

"My mom just landed a tenure-track job at the university. Physics. She's really psyched about it."

"Physics? Your mom's a scientist?" I said, interested enough to forget my discomfort for a second.

"Bailey's a scientist too," Simone piped up. "Our bio teacher says she'll probably win the Nobel Prize someday."

I shot her a murderous look. Mr. Ba *so* hadn't said that.

"Really? Cool." Logan gave me another of those appraising blue-eyed looks.

"Um . . ." As I was figuring out whether it was actually scientifically possible to die of embarrassment, three or four people burst into Eats, laughing and talking loudly. College rugby players, I guessed, based on their clothes and the mud covering every inch of them from hair to cleats. Eats was a favorite stop after sports practices thanks to our Belly Buster specials.

"Suz!" one of the rugby players shouted. "Feed us, woman!"

Susannah rolled her eyes and smiled at the player and his friends, then glanced at me. "Think I'm going to need a little help back here, Bailey," she said.

"I've got it!" Simone exclaimed before I could answer. "I'll go make sandwiches. You stay right here, Bails."

I opened my mouth to protest, but it was too late. She was already scooting behind the counter. Simone worked at Eats part-time in the summer, so Susannah just nodded as she pushed past, heading for the kitchen.

As the rugby players clustered around the register, Logan and I stepped back. "This seems like a cool place," he said. "So your family has owned it for a long time, huh?"

"Ages. Since before my mom was born, actually." I was glad he seemed to be ignoring Simone's ridiculous Nobel Prize comment. Still, I couldn't resist turning the topic back to science. "So your mom's a physics prof? And she went to MIT?"

"Yeah. She and Dad met there as undergrads. He's a science guy too—paleontology. He's been working on a book while Mom climbs her way up the academic ranks."

"Works her way up?" I was distracted by the way his lips went a little bit crooked when he smiled, though I wasn't sure why. I didn't usually notice stuff like that about random strangers unless I was doing research for a human-genetics project or something.

"Yeah," he said. "First she was finishing up her PhD; then she had a bunch of nontenured jobs and stuff. So we've lived in a bunch of different places."

"Really? Like where?"

Logan leaned against an empty table. "We just moved here from Switzerland. Before that was Boston—we were only there for a year—and then Tokyo and California. We also spent a couple of summers in Botswana for Dad's research. And one in Singapore for Mom's."

"Wow." I wondered what it would be like to live that way—moving to a new city or country every couple of years.

"So what about you?" Logan asked. "Have you always lived here?"

"Uh-huh." I shrugged. "Totally boring, right?"

"Oh, I don't know." He flashed me that off-kilter smile. "There's something kind of nice about knowing where you belong. Maybe I'll finally find out what that's like. It looks like this time my family might actually stay put for a while."

"Oh." I'd observed Simone talking to guys for long enough to know that she'd probably have a flirty comeback for a comment like that. Me? Not so much. For a moment I'd almost forgotten I was talking to a guy. Now it all came crashing back, and Logan and I stood there staring at each other for what felt like forever but was probably only a few seconds.

"So," he said at last, "what's the local high school like? I'm starting there tomorrow, and I could use any tips you can give me."

"It's okay, I guess." I tried to think of something witty to say but came up empty. "Um, just a typical high school."

The door flew open again. This time at least half a dozen more rugby players poured in. At the same time, Susannah hit the little silver bell by the register.

"Morse!" she called out. "Order's up!"

"That's me." Logan glanced over. "I should get going, I guess. Looks like things are getting busy."

"Yeah. They probably need me to help back there." I stepped aside as a rugby player barreled past, shouting something about a bacon craving.

"Okay." Logan hesitated, shooting another look in Susannah's direction, then turning back to me. "I'll see you at school tomorrow, right, Bailey? You and—um, your friend."

I blinked. Had my ears deceived me, or had this cute guy actually remembered my name—and forgotten Simone's? That had never happened before.

"Yeah," I said just as Susannah shouted my name, sounding frazzled.

"Guess you'd better go. See you." With one last smile, Logan eased his way through the shifting mass of rugby players to grab the big white bag with his name scrawled on it. I noticed there was a smiley face drawn in the *O*—Simone's work, obviously.

Seconds later he was on his way out. I watched him go, feeling oddly disappointed. I figured it was probably because I hadn't learned more about his mother. It was always cool to hear about successful women in science. It gave me hope that my dreams of becoming a biomedical researcher someday could actually come true.

Simone made a beeline for me when I entered the kitchen. "Well?" she demanded. "Tell me everything!"

"Everything?" I grabbed an apron from the hook by the door and tied it around my waist. "That'll take a while."

"Ha-ha, very funny. You know what I mean." She jabbed

me in the arm with a latex-gloved finger. "Logan. You. What happened after I left? Did he ask you out?"

"What? No!" I shot a look at my dad and Uncle Rick to make sure they hadn't overheard. "Are you crazy?"

"Girls!" Uncle Rick's voice rang out from the other end of the huge stainless-steel table, where he was rapidly assembling a pair of roast-beef subs. "More work, less gossip, please."

"*You're* crazy if you missed the way Logan was checking you out," Simone hissed.

There was no more time for talking. Which was just as well, since I had no idea what to say to *that*.

Chapter ⬛ Two

Whenever anyone asked how Simone and I became best friends, I told them it worked on the same scientific principle as one of those school IDs that unlocked the gym doors when you held it close enough to the sensor. Proximity. We'd been friends since we were tiny tots because we lived right next door to each other.

Actually, that was only part of the reason. The other part was that our mothers had been best friends since they were teenagers themselves. I doubted they'd started out as different as Simone and me, but their lives had definitely gone in different directions for a while. My mom married her high school sweetheart, graduated from the local university, then went right to work in the family business (dragging Dad in with her). Meanwhile, Simone's mom went off to college in California. She spent her junior year abroad in Paris, then went back to France after she graduated. She lived there for a couple of years, and in the process fell madly in love with a Frenchman of Algerian descent. They got married, she dragged him back here to live, and the rest was history.

I'd always found that story awfully romantic, even though I wasn't usually the romantic type. I liked the idea that there really was a big, wide world out there beyond my boring little hometown. Anytime I doubted that, I just had to look at Simone's dad. Or, better yet, listen to him. Even after almost twenty years in the US, his accent was atrocious.

"*Bonjour*, Bailey," he greeted me when I let myself into the Amrou house through the screen door on Sunday evening. "Simone is in the kitchen helping to wash up after supper. Oh, and tell your mama that her apple pie was *délicieux*!" He kissed his fingertips, just like someone in a cheesy French film. Only he wasn't doing it ironically—he actually meant it. I loved when he did stuff like that, even though it embarrassed Simone sometimes.

"Thanks, Mr. A," I told him with a smile. "I'll tell her."

I headed toward the kitchen. Simone and I hadn't had much chance to talk since the rugby invasion earlier that day. First we'd both stayed busy making sandwiches and serving customers. Then Simone's mom had called to tell her to head home for dinner (and to bring a pie from the bakery case).

Simone heard me coming. "I thought you'd never get here!"

she complained, tossing aside the dishrag she was using to dry a pan. "Mom's forcing me to be her scullery maid."

"Her what?" I shot a look at Mrs. Amrou, who was dunking a pair of wine glasses into the sink. Simone and her mother didn't look much alike except for their matching sharp chins and tiny ears. Mrs. Amrou was petite and pale, with auburn hair and a smattering of freckles across her upturned nose.

"You'd better not complain about washing a few pots and pans, m'dear," Mrs. Amrou told her daughter. She glanced over at me and winked. "Otherwise I'm sure Bailey's folks could find you a nice full-time job washing up at Eats."

"Okay, okay." Simone set the pan on the drying rack. "But if Bails doesn't help me figure out how to pass this test tomorrow, that might be my only option for employment someday."

"Fine." Mrs. Amrou chuckled. "You're excused."

"Great." Simone grabbed a pair of sodas out of the fridge and tossed one to me. "It's a gorgeous night. Let's study in the tree house."

Soon we were climbing the rickety homemade ladder leading up to the tree house. It had been our spot since the third grade, when our dads had helped us build it. It was basically just a big wooden box tucked into a crook of the ancient oak that stood on the property line between our two houses, shading Mr. Amrou's hammock on their side and Mom's hostas on ours. When we were younger, Simone and I used to wait up there until her dad fell asleep in the hammock, then have contests to see who could drop a piece of popcorn or a potato chip or whatever and have it land on his face. Good times.

Simone dumped her books on the rough plank floor, then flopped onto one of the big overstuffed floor cushions we'd made in our eighth-grade family-science class (which didn't actually have much to do with science at all, by the way, unless you counted cooking and sewing as science, which I didn't).

"So," she said. "I've totally got the scoop on your new boyfriend."

"What?" I grabbed her biology textbook, flipping through it until I found the chapter on RNA. "Hey, aren't we supposed to be studying? You know, so you don't flunk out of bio class and become a professional dishwasher?"

"That can wait." Those three words pretty much summed up Simone's philosophy on life and homework, at least when boys were involved. "I texted the girls as soon as I could to see if any of them knew anything about Logan."

"The girls" were our other friends. Well, they'd started out as Simone's other friends, really. They were mostly like her—popular and confident and pretty. But they seemed to accept me as their token science-geek friend, so it all worked out.

"What did they say?" I couldn't help asking.

Simone's eyes lit up. "See? I *knew* you liked him!" she crowed. "I mean, since when do you care about the latest boy gossip? Even a super-hot, super-smart boy who was practically drooling all over you?"

"Give me a break," I muttered, folding a corner of a page up and down where Simone had dog-eared it. "If you don't want to tell me what you found out . . ."

"No, no, I'm telling you." She scrolled through her phone as she talked, checking her messages. "None of them knew a thing about him yet, but they were all intrigued."

A horrible thought occurred to me. "Wait. You didn't, like, tell them I'm madly in love with this guy or something, did you?"

"Of course not!" She sounded offended. "That's *your* news to share—when you're ready."

"Which will be approximately never," I said. "Because it's not true."

"Whatever you say." She smirked, then glanced down at her phone again. "Okay, so the only one who'd even vaguely heard about Logan was Taylor. She confirmed that he's a sophomore like us, only she thought he was a girl."

"She did?" That was pretty ditzy even for Taylor, who didn't always take in all of life's little details. She was actually pretty smart—she'd written a poem last year in English class that had ended up winning all sorts of awards and getting published in the university's literary magazine. But at times she seemed to be trying to live up to the dumb-blonde stereotype, even though her hair color came straight out of a bottle.

"Yeah. Apparently her mom mentioned there'd be a new kid starting in our class soon, but with all the background screaming, Taylor thought the name was Lauren or something, not Logan."

That made more sense. Taylor's mom worked in the front office at school, and Taylor had twin toddler half brothers who talked constantly and at the top of their lungs.

"What about Ling?" I asked. "Her dad must know Logan's mom, right? He's on the hiring committee at the university."

"Yeah, I thought of that too." Simone shrugged. "She was clueless, but promised to dig up the dirt."

I nodded. If there was any dirt to be dug up, Ling would find it. The girl could be relentless—verging on ruthless.

Simone peered at her phone's screen. "Wait, Megan just texted me back." She scanned the message. "She doesn't know anything about Logan. But she's dying to check him out."

"Yeah, I bet." Megan was one of the prettiest girls in school—and one of the most boy crazy.

Simone lowered her phone and eyed me. "Is that jealousy I sense over there?" she teased. "I knew it was love at first sight!"

"Don't be silly. There's no such thing." I hesitated. "Or at least, scientists say what most people call love at first sight is actually a mostly involuntary physiological reaction that comes from the release of adrenaline and dopamine and some other chemicals in the brain based on a quick assessment of a potential mate's facial features."

"Very romantic." Simone grinned. "Is all that mumbo gumbo true?"

"It's mumbo *jumbo*. And yes—I read an article about it in one of the science journals a couple of months ago."

"So is that how you felt when you first laid eyes on Logan?" She waggled her eyebrows. "Like you just really, really dug his facial features? Or what?"

"I don't know. It was weird."

"You're going to have to be more specific."

I picked at the edge of the textbook page, thinking back to seeing Logan walk in the door. "Usually I don't think about guys that much. I mean, what's the point?"

Simone sighed. "Not this again."

I shrugged. What could I say? She knew my philosophy about guys and dating. I'd always figured that logically, there wasn't much point in wasting time on high school romance. For one thing, most of the guys at school were much more interested in sports and movies and stuff than anything intellectual, including science. Meanwhile I was all about studying hard so I could get into a great college (preferably MIT, though I knew that was a long shot). Guys tended to find that weird, apparently, since they seemed to be in no hurry to ask me out.

But that was okay; I was in no hurry either. I figured I had much better odds of meeting a smart guy, one I had something in common with, once I got to college. Or if not there, then in med school for sure.

"Anyway, it doesn't matter," I told Simone, pushing her textbook toward her. "Guys like Logan don't notice me, remember? He was probably just being polite, maybe hoping I'd put in a good word for him with you."

"No way." Simone sounded sure of herself. "He barely looked at me."

"You're delusional." I chewed my lower lip thoughtfully. "I just wish I knew why I reacted that way to this particular guy. Maybe I'm deficient in iron or something. I've read that can cause mental confusion."

She ignored my hypothesis. "When did it start?" she asked. "You reacting to Logan, I mean. Was it as soon as he walked in the door?"

I thought about it for a second. "I think so. I definitely noticed right away that he was pretty cute. That's just neurotransmitters at work, though."

"What? Wait, never mind, don't start up with all that again." She leaned forward. "So then how did you feel?"

"Well . . . intrigued, I guess? Like I wanted him to come over and talk to us, but at the same time I wanted to run away and hide." I shook my head. "Totally illogical."

"And then when you were talking to him . . . ?"

"It was—mostly cool, I guess. I mean, you were there—you heard me spewing gibberish as usual. But he didn't laugh or roll his eyes or anything. He was actually pretty easy to talk to." I shrugged. "At least for a guy."

"I have a diagnosis for you, Dr. Myers." Simone leaned back against the tree house wall, looking very serious. "I'm afraid you've come down with a bad case of . . . sparks."

I wrinkled my nose. "What?"

"Sparks." She smiled. "That's when two people hit it off. You know—chemistry."

"We don't take that until next year," I joked weakly, glancing at her bio book. "Anyway, even if I do have a case of sparks, I'm sure it's totally one-sided."

"I don't think so. But how do you know until you go for it? What have you got to lose?"

Typical Simone. "Kind of a lot, really." I started ticking items off on my fingers. "My dignity, my self-respect, my lunch . . ."

"No, seriously. It's not like you're throwing yourself at some random guy. He was really into you. I guarantee it."

I thought about that for a second. Simone was really good at this boy-girl stuff. She'd had her first "date"—sharing a juice box with Zach Harasta—way back in first grade, and had never looked back. All our friends went to her for advice about guys. Whether they took that advice or not, Simone usually turned out to be right in the end. Could she be right about this?

"No way," I answered myself aloud. "We're making a mountain out of a molehill."

Simone chugged her soda. "We'll just have to see what happens at school tomorrow," she said, wiping her mouth. "And don't worry, I know you're new to this. I'll be with you every step of the way, helping you figure it out."

"Figure what out?" My little sister's face suddenly appeared over the lip of the tree house doorway. "What are you guys talking about?"

"Ash!" I scowled at her. "What are you doing here?"

She smirked. "Simone's mom sent me. I'm supposed to spy on you and see if you guys are studying or goofing off."

Simone rolled her eyes. "Great job, Jamesina Bond. You're super stealthy."

"Whatever." That was Ashley's favorite word lately. "So are you studying or what? I have to go back and tell her or she won't give me a piece of pie."

"Yes, we're studying." I grabbed Simone's textbook and flipped through the pages. "See? Study study study."

"Okay. See you." Ash's head disappeared. A moment later we heard a soft thump as she jumped the last few feet to the ground.

Simone checked her watch and gulped, suddenly looking panicky. "Oh, wow, it's getting late. We'd better start studying for real."

"Agreed." I plunked the textbook down in front of her. I was tired of thinking about the whole Logan encounter anyway—it made my head hurt. "Now, tell me what you know about RNA. . . ."

Chapter ● Three

"Bailey! Over here!"

I paused and scanned the crowded hallway, finally spotting Ling and our other friend Zoe walking toward me. Zoe was waving both arms over her head, which was actually pretty dramatic given that she was almost six feet tall and built like an Amazon. It was no wonder she was already getting scouted by the basketball and volleyball coaches at the university. Or that her nickname around the athletic department was Zoena, Warrior Princess.

Beside Zoe, Ling looked extra petite and girly. As usual, everything about her was sleek and stylish, from the beaded band holding back her long, straight black hair to her dark-wash skinny jeans.

"Hey," she greeted me, her expertly lined eyes lingering only momentarily on my face before darting off, scanning the crowds for something more interesting. "Where's Simone?"

"She texted to say she wasn't taking the bus—her dad's dropping her off on his way to work so she can spend more time cramming for the bio test." The three of us drifted over to our usual pre-homeroom meeting spot between the school bulletin board and the water fountain.

"Oh." Ling pulled out her phone, checked her messages, then dropped it back into her designer purse. "So what's up? Did you guys hear about those seniors who got busted at a frat party up at the college?"

"I know, right?" Zoe's eyes lit up. "My neighbor told me all about it. She was there, but she left just in time . . ."

As they chattered on about the latest frat-party scandal, I shifted my backpack to my other shoulder and glanced around, hoping Simone would get there soon. Yes, Ling and Zoe were my friends too. But even after hanging out with them since middle school, I still wasn't sure we had that much in common. While most people at school probably thought of me as part of the popular crowd, I considered myself more like popularity adjacent. Ling and Zoe and the others seemed to accept me just fine, maybe even like me, but I was convinced it was all because of Simone. We came as a package deal.

"So what about this new guy?"

I blinked, realizing Zoe was addressing me. "Huh?" I said.

"Oh yeah, Simone's mystery man. I asked my dad about him."
Ling pulled out a tube of lip gloss, slicking it on as she talked.
"Dad said the guy's mom is some rising star in the science world or
something, and the university was totally geeked to snag her." She
shrugged her slim shoulders and eyed me, one corner of her newly
glossed lips turning up in a half smile. "Sounds more like your
kind of guy than Simone's, right? Science isn't exactly her thing."

"Um . . ." I wasn't sure what to say to that. As I tried not to
meet Ling's eye, I finally spotted my best friend pushing through
the front doors. "Look, here comes Simone."

Simone reached us a moment later, breathless and with spots
of pink on her cheeks. Two guys were trailing along behind her—
her boyfriend, Matt, and his best friend, Darius.

"I am so going to fail that bio test!" Simone exclaimed dramatically, grabbing my arm. "I studied so hard this morning that
my eyes are crossing. And I'm *still* not sure what the difference is
between DNA and RNA."

Zoe punched her lightly on the shoulder. "Toldja you should've
taken earth science instead, like me."

"Thanks a lot." Simone rolled her eyes. "Very helpful, Z."

Matt stepped up and slung an arm around her shoulders.
"Chin up, babe," he said with a grin. "Dumb girls are totally hot."

She shrugged his arm off and shoved him away. "Not funny,
Mr. Neanderthal."

The rest of us laughed. Matt liked to tease Simone by pretending to be some macho jerk. But he was actually pretty cool.

It was amazing. As soon as a guy started going out with one of my friends, I suddenly found him a lot easier to talk to. Like the pressure was off, I guess.

"Okay, so now we know why Simone biffed every play at kickball practice on Saturday," Darius put in. "She was distracted thinking about science." His big grin seemed to light up the hallway as he glanced at me. "Usually that's Bailey's gig, right? You two didn't switch brains without telling us, did you?"

"I wish," Simone said. "If I had Bailey's brain, I wouldn't be so worried about this stupid test."

I just laughed along with the others, feeling a little flustered. Darius was one of the most popular guys at school. Our group had always been friendly with him, but he'd started hanging out with us a lot more once Simone and Matt got together.

"We'll *all* need to step it up at kickball practice this weekend," Zoe said, getting that super-intense-competitive-athlete look in her greenish-hazel eyes. "It's the last one before the Co-Ed/Lo-Ed championship, and we have a title to defend!" She pumped her fist for emphasis.

The Co-Ed/Lo-Ed kickball tournament was a long-running tradition in our town. Although "tournament" was probably the wrong word, since there were really only two teams involved—one from the college (the Co-Eds) and one from our high school (the Lo-Eds). We played each other once a month all year, culminating in a big championship game that took place the Saturday of the Spring Thing. Simone and I were on the Lo-Ed team, along with Matt and Darius and Zoe. Ling preferred to cheer us on from the sidelines, with our other friends Taylor and Megan.

"You aren't letting that traitor cousin of yours steal our plays, are you, B?" Matt gave me a playful poke on the arm.

"Don't worry, I'm guarding our team secrets with my life," I joked back.

That was another thing about the rivalry. It was often complicated when someone graduated from the Lo-Ed team to the Co-Ed one, like Susannah had when she went off to college.

"We don't have to worry about Bails—she's a vault," Simone put in. "Now, Darius and his big mouth, on the other hand . . ."

"Hey!" Darius pretended to be insulted. "I haven't told my brother a thing. I even moved into a tent in the backyard in case I talk in my sleep."

"In case?" Matt smirked. "Dude, I'd be shocked if you *didn't* talk in your sleep. I mean, you never stop talking while you're awake."

As the two guys got into a mock shoving match, I spotted Megan and Taylor coming toward us. Megan was always hard to miss. As if her pretty face, curvy figure, and gorgeous pale skin weren't enough, it was all topped off with a head of long, wavy, dramatic red hair that looked like it had come straight out of a shampoo ad. Most of the guys at school called her Megan the Magnificent.

Taylor faded into the background a bit beside Megan, just like I always did when I was with Simone—not that I'd ever tell

Taylor that. She didn't take that sort of thing well, mostly because she was much harder on herself than anyone else could ever be, especially when it came to her weight and the little mole under her left eye.

"We spotted the new guy," Taylor said when they reached us.

Megan nodded, her green eyes flashing with excitement. "He just came out of the office. Come on, let's get over there before he gets lost in the crowd!"

"Right behind you." Ling reached up to check her hair. "What's the verdict? Is he as cute as Simone says?"

"What, don't you trust my taste?" Simone said with a grin. "Come on, Bails. Let's go say hi to Logan."

Not giving me a chance to respond, she grabbed my hand and dragged me along. Everyone else followed, including the two guys. I realized my heart was pounding as if I'd just run a homer in kickball. Why? Was this another symptom of the mysterious sparks disease Simone had diagnosed me with?

We rounded the corner into the administration hall. I spotted Logan right away, and immediately had a flip-flopping stomach to add to my list of symptoms. He was leaning against the wall outside the main office, dressed in well-worn jeans, with a backpack slung over one shoulder, studying a slip of paper. When I glanced at the other girls, I could see that all of them were checking him out. Ling's dark eyes were narrowed with interest, while Taylor's practically bulged out of her head. Megan and Zoe were trading an impressed glance.

I felt another yank on my arm as Simone hurried forward. "Logan!" she called, waving with her free hand. "Hi! How's it going?"

Logan glanced up, almost immediately breaking into that slightly crooked smile. "Hey! How's it going, Bailey? And, um . . . sorry." He flashed Simone a helpless smile. "Help me out here—is it Cindy?"

"Close!" Simone giggled. "It's Simone. So, welcome to our lovely school."

"Thanks. Seems pretty cool here so far." He shot me a grin. "Definitely a typical American high school, just like Bailey told me."

"Yeah." I desperately searched my mind for something witty to say. "Uh, no MIT shirt today, huh?"

Okay, not so witty. But he chuckled anyway. "Nah, it was pretty gross by the time I finished helping Dad lug all his filing cabinets up the stairs into his new home office."

"So where do you live, Logan?" Ling asked. She and the others had stepped forward to join us by now. "It *is* Logan, right? I'm Ling. Simone and Bailey told us all about running into you yesterday."

Ugh! Why did she have to say that? Now Logan was probably going to think I'd been blabbing about him all over town. *It was Simone!* I wanted to shout. *Just Simone! She's the one who's been gossiping about you—not me!*

But of course I didn't say a thing. Just stood there like a dork as everyone traded introductions. Meanwhile I couldn't seem to stop staring at Logan. I was pretty sure he noticed too—I caught his eyes sliding toward me a couple of times. Probably wondering whether I was dangerous or just weird.

"So when did you move here, Logan?" Megan asked.

"This weekend—we flew in from Zurich just in time to meet the moving van that brought our stuff out of storage in Boston." Logan didn't seem fazed at all by being interrogated by more than half a dozen near strangers. "So this town's still brand-new to me. Luckily, our new neighbors already filled us in on all the cool local spots. Like College Avenue Eats, for instance." He turned and smiled at me. "By the way, my parents loved the sandwiches, Bailey. They said to give their compliments to the chef."

"That would be me!" Simone dropped into a little curtsy. "But I can't take much credit—Bailey taught me everything I know. She's super talented in all kinds of ways."

"Stop," I muttered. Seeing that Logan was still smiling at me for some reason, I felt another flutter of those sparks, though I did my best to shove them aside. "Anyway, I'm glad you liked the food. Or your parents did. Um, whatever."

"If you liked the sandwiches, you should totally try the cupcakes," Taylor put in. "They're to die for. I'm, like, totally addicted to the banana ones."

"Sounds good. I'll have to check them out." Logan was still watching me. Was I acting *that* weird? Did they not have geeky girls in Switzerland? Then again, maybe it was scientific interest—he could be wondering why my face was so red that I looked like some kind of human-lobster hybrid. Not that that was scientifically possible as far as I knew.

"Is that your schedule?" Ling sidled closer to Logan and peered at the paper he was holding, "What homeroom do you have?"

"Um . . ." Logan checked the paper. "It says Garcia, room twelve?"

"Cool! That's my homeroom." Matt offered him a fist bump. "Simone's, too."

"And mine," Megan put in quickly.

Logan glanced at me. "What about you, Bailey?"

"Me?" I stared at him uncertainly. "What about me?"

Simone giggled and poked me in the shoulder. "Snap out of it, Myers!" She tilted her head and smiled at Logan. "You'll have to forgive Bailey. She's so smart that sometimes her brain doesn't compute our lowly human language."

The others chuckled, and I forced a smile. But inside I was cringing. Great. Now Logan was going to think I was some kind of supernerd snob on top of everything else.

"Uh, I was just wondering what homeroom you're in," Logan told me, his smile wavering slightly. "Are you with us in room twelve?"

"No, she's in nineteen with me." Ling checked her watch. "Speaking of which, Bailey, we'd better get over there. Mr. Chance will flip his lid if I'm late one more time, and I have better things to do than sit in detention this afternoon. See you soon, Logan. Later, guys."

"Yeah, uh, bye," I mumbled, turning to follow her.

"Later, Bailey," Logan said. "You too, Ling."

As soon as we rounded the corner, Ling glanced over at me. "So you and Simone were right—he's *interesting*." That was one of her favorite words. It meant she hadn't made her mind up yet about Logan, though she was intrigued enough to pay attention. "So what did you guys talk about when he came into the deli yesterday?"

"I don't know." My mind felt numb as I stumbled along next to her. I'd hoped the sparks thing from yesterday had just been a fluke, but if anything it had been even worse just now. "Not that much. He wasn't there very long."

"Too bad." Ling pursed her lips thoughtfully. "We should get him to sit with us at lunch. Then we can get the scoop."

I gulped. If Logan sat with us at lunch, I wasn't sure the butterflies in my stomach would allow me to eat. . . .

Wait. What was wrong with me, anyway? So one cute guy had smiled at me a few times—that was no reason to go all fuzzy-headed and goofy. Especially today, with that important bio test coming up. That test was something that could affect my entire future, unlike some guy who barely knew I existed.

That thought snapped me out of it, at least mostly. Doing my best to forget about Logan, sparks, and any related silliness, I followed Ling into homeroom.

Chapter ⬤ Four

'd almost forgotten about Logan by the time the bell rang to end first period.

Okay, not really. But I was *trying* to forget about him. Watching him chat with my friends that morning, I'd realized something. If he'd moved around as much as he said, he was probably used to being nice to everyone so he could make friends quickly at each new school. I shouldn't assume the way he'd acted with me was anything special—that I was any different from anyone else he'd ever met. Or that he was feeling any of those crazy sparks-like feelings that kept plaguing me.

It was hard to remember that, though, when I saw him coming out of a classroom across the hall. He spotted me at the same moment.

"Bailey! Hey!" he called, raising a hand in greeting.

He hurried over and fell into step beside me. "Hi, Logan," I said, doing my best to sound casual and normal. "How's it going so far?"

"Not too bad. Survived first period okay." He pulled his schedule out of his back pocket and consulted it. "I've got art next. What about you?"

"I have art too." My heart gave a little leap. Stupid heart! Hadn't it heard anything I was just thinking? "Um, I can show you where it is if you want," I added.

"Cool, thanks." He leaned a little closer, nudging my shoulder lightly with his. "It'll be nice to have a friendly face in there. I didn't know a soul in geometry."

Okay, the sparks were back, big-time. I couldn't help being really, really glad that the only elective that had fit in my schedule this semester was art.

"The art room's this way," I said, gesturing vaguely down the hall.

"So what's the class like?" he asked as we walked.

"It's okay." I dodged a couple of giggling freshman. "Small. Kind of weird sometimes."

That was an understatement. Ms. Blumenkranz, the art teacher, was a world-class wacko. She was always coming up with bizarre new projects, and she gave As to anyone who made an effort. Which was a good thing, since I could barely draw a stick figure, and I needed to keep my GPA up if I wanted to get any academic scholarships someday. Which I did. My family earned too much to qualify for financial aid, but not nearly enough to pay tuition at a top school like MIT.

"Here we are," I told Logan as we stepped into the art room, which was big and sunny. Instead of normal desks, there were tables of various shapes and sizes scattered through the room.

None of my close friends were in the class, so I usually sat with Gabi and Gwen, a couple of girls I'd known since kindergarten. Gwen was sort of a goth pixie—she was tiny and sarcastic with huge gray eyes and an incredibly vast wardrobe of black clothes. Gabi was taller and plumper and liked to wear colorful layers of weirdness she'd put together herself from thrift-store finds. Both of them were into music and theater and stuff like that, and neither of them seemed to care how strange most people thought they were. Basically, they were nothing like my regular crew, but they always made me laugh, and I never felt awkward or unworthy around them like I sometimes did even with my own best friends.

When I walked in with Logan, the two of them were in their usual seats at our usual table, a massive square butcher block that had probably started life as a kitchen island. Today Gabi had a huge, floppy gingham bow tying back her frizzy blond hair, while Gwen was drawing a fake tattoo on her arm with some colored markers. I shot a quick glance at Logan, wondering how he'd react to the pair. Would he think they were weird? Would he think *I* was weird for hanging out with them?

And so what if he did? I was annoyed with myself for even

thinking about it. "I usually sit over here," I told him. "There's a free seat, you know, if you want it."

"Sure. If that's okay."

"Yeah. Ms. Blumenkranz lets us sit wherever we want." I gestured toward the teacher, who was talking to another student at the front of the room.

Gabi and Gwen stared at Logan as we sat down across from them. "New kid, huh?" Gwen said, capping her marker and tossing it into the big bin of art supplies in the center of the table.

"Way to state the obvious." Gabi laughed. "Next thing we know, you'll be noticing that the sky is blue."

"It is?" Gwen widened her charcoal-lined eyes dramatically and stared up at the ceiling.

Logan chuckled. "Hi," he said. "I'm Logan."

"I'm Gabi, and this is Gwen." Gabi stuck out her hand for him to shake. She and Gwen didn't seem the least bit intimidated or impressed by Logan's good looks, which surprised me a little. Then again, maybe it shouldn't have. Not much fazed those two.

"Logan, huh? Cool name." Gwen looked him up and down appraisingly. "You ever do any acting?"

"Leave him alone," I told her with a grin. Then I glanced at Logan. "These guys are seriously into theater. If you don't watch out, they'll drag you off and start putting makeup on you."

"Real men wear makeup," Gabi informed me.

At that moment Ms. Blumenkranz clapped her hands. The

art teacher was almost as old as my great-aunt Ellen, though much taller and slimmer. She always wore long, flowy dresses and tons of chunky jewelry, and her close-cropped hair was dyed a vibrant shade of green.

"Pipe down, young *artistes*," she said, putting a fancy French flourish on the last word. "It's time to discuss today's creation. I'd like you to explore the ways we can use the simplest of materials to create something deeply meaningful on a personal level." She walked over to a box sitting on her desk and pulled something out. "This is a box of toothpicks."

"Oh, lordy," Gwen said under her breath.

Ms. Blumenkranz didn't hear her. "I want you each to create a self-portrait," she went on. "It can take any form you like—the more creative the better. The only rule is that you can use nothing but toothpicks, glue, and paint." She dug out more boxes of toothpicks. "Let's begin!"

A few kids gave playful whoops. Gabi stuck her fingers in her mouth and let out a loud wolf whistle. Ms. Blumenkranz just chuckled and started passing out toothpick boxes.

"Okay, this is a new one for me," Logan whispered, leaning so close I could feel his breath on my cheek. "Is she serious? I've never made toothpick art before. At least not since kindergarten."

"Y-yeah." I was embarrassed to note that my voice trembled at having him so close. Luckily, he sat back as Ms. Blumenkranz approached our table.

"Ah, you must be the new boy. Mr. Morse, isn't it?" She

beamed at Logan. "Welcome, welcome! I hope you're embracing your new reality here at our fair school."

"Sure, yeah." Logan sounded confused but polite. "Bailey has been helping me settle in, so that helps."

I had? That was news to me. As far as I knew, all I'd done was walk him to this class. Oh, and make a complete idiot out of myself in front of him. Multiple times.

"Wonderful." The teacher patted me on the shoulder. I tried not to wince as her enormous rings slammed into me. "Carry on! I look forward to seeing your creation, Mr. Morse—it will help me get to know you better." She raised a finger and winked. "And perhaps it will help you get to know yourself better too."

She dropped several boxes of toothpicks on our table, then moved on. "She's . . . interesting," Logan murmured.

"Yeah." I busied myself with carefully opening the lid of my toothpick box, then picking a few of the tiny sticks of wood out and setting them neatly in front of me. Maybe that would distract me from the memory of his breath on my face. . . .

Across the way, Gabi had already dumped her toothpicks into a messy pile in front of her. "But seriously, Logan," she said, picking up right where she and Gwen had left off before. "Can you sing at all? We're casting *Camelot* next week—sign-up sheet's on the bulletin board. You've got the perfect look for Lancelot."

Gwen snorted. "Are you kidding? James would slit the throat of anyone who tried to wrestle that part away from him."

Logan gave an exaggerated shudder and grabbed his own

neck. "In that case, no thanks, ladies," he said. "Besides, I'm practically tone-deaf."

"Too bad." Gabi shrugged and turned to Gwen. "Guess we're stuck with James."

Gwen held up a toothpick and studied it thoughtfully. "Yeah. Which means we'll need a really short girl to play Guenevere."

"I can play short." Gabi hunched down in her chair. "Although I'm not sure even *I* can act well enough to pretend I'm in love with James. . . ."

With that, they were off and running on their usual theater gossip. Normally I enjoyed listening—it was fun to peek into what was going on outside my little circle of friends. Gabi and Gwen were obviously just as passionate about the theater as I was about science, and I could respect that.

But today, all I could focus on was Logan. He was fiddling with his toothpicks, rolling several between his fingers.

"Any ideas?" I picked up a couple of toothpicks myself and stared at them. "Maybe I could turn these into molecular structure or something. That could be like a self-portrait. Sort of."

"You're really into science, huh?" Logan asked.

I shot him a nervous look. "Yeah. How did you know that?" It came out a little more accusatory than I'd intended.

Luckily, he didn't seem to notice. "Your friend said you want to go to MIT, and you seemed excited when you heard my parents are both scientists." He smiled. "And you just said you wanted to make a molecular thingy as your self-portrait."

Oh. Right. At least now I knew he hadn't been totally blinded by Simone's beauty while I was talking yesterday.

"Okay, yeah, I admit it, that's me—total science geek," I said, trying to turn the whole thing into a joke. That was usually how I handled the topic when it came up with people I didn't know very well. "My parents say they have no idea where it came from. Apparently, my dad barely passed chemistry when he was in high school, and Mom only ever paid attention to learning enough science to mix dough properly."

Logan laughed. "Pass me the glue?"

"Sure." I grabbed a bottle of Elmer's out of the supply box. As he took it, his fingers brushed mine, but I tried not to notice that. Even though my whole hand started to tingle.

Or maybe that was all in my mind. I couldn't think of a single physiological reason that a light touch between two people with no obvious skin maladies would cause that sort of reaction.

"Anyway," I said a little too loudly, "tell me about *your* parents. You said they met at MIT?"

"Yeah. Apparently, Mom was doing some kind of experiment for her organic chemistry lab, and Dad bumbled past and broke her test tube or something. After he apologized, he offered to help her rerun the lab—then he took her out to some lecture on superconductors. And the rest was history." He grinned. "Just your typical whirlwind romance, right?"

I stared into space, picturing it. A quiet laboratory late at night. An accomplished young coed encountering a devastatingly intelligent and adorable young nerd-hunk. Wasn't that almost exactly the kind of romantic moment I'd pictured happening to me someday? The way I might meet my future Dr. Right—a guy more likely to suggest a date to a science lecture than a basketball game? It sounded perfect—well, minus the broken test tube, anyway.

Suddenly realizing that Logan was still looking at me, I snapped back to reality. How long had I spaced out for? I felt a hot blush creeping up over my cheeks.

"Um, sure, romantic," I muttered, ducking my head and focusing intently on my toothpicks. I was hardly aware of what I was doing as I rapidly started squirting glue here and there, sticking things together without a plan.

He stayed silent for a moment. Across the table I could hear Gwen and Gabi arguing over whether the movie version of *Camelot* was better or worse than the miniseries. Finally I peeked over and saw that Logan was focused on his project too. I caught his eyes shooting sideways toward me for a second, but he didn't turn his head.

Oops. See, this was why I didn't usually try to get involved in this boy-girl stuff. Up until now, Logan had actually been pretty easy to talk to, almost like a normal nonguy person. Now, just like that, the air between us had gone all awkward. But why? What had I said?

Before I could figure it out, Ms. Blumenkranz swooped down on our table again. "How goes it, young *artistes*?" she asked. "Are you creating magic?"

"Definitely." Gwen gestured at her project like a used-car salesman. "*Voilà!* Self-portrait in black."

The teacher peered at Gwen's creation, a jumble of toothpicks with black paint splashed over it. "Fascinating," she said. "Very dark, almost seething with meaning. I can see your spirit in it, Gwen. Good work."

"Mine's not ready yet." Gabi covered up her own pile of toothpicks. "Look at the others first, okay?"

"Of course. Mr. Morse? Have you prepared a suitable introduction for us into your innermost thoughts and feelings?" The teacher smiled at him.

"I guess so." Logan pushed his toothpick art forward. "Here it is."

"Oh, my!" The teacher sounded impressed.

As much attention as I'd been paying—and trying *not* to pay—to Logan himself, I'd barely glanced at his project. Now I saw that he'd somehow fashioned his toothpicks into the shape of a running figure. It sprang out of a simple square toothpick base, balanced on one foot, the other leg reaching forward and both arms pumping.

"Wow, cool." Gwen stood and leaned across the table for a better look. "That actually looks like you!" She shrugged. "Or, you know, at least like a person."

"I call it *Constant Motion.*" Logan carefully adjusted the figure's left arm. "That's kind of how my life has always been. You know—because my family moves around a lot."

"Fabulous!" Ms. Blumenkranz clapped her hands, making her bracelets jingle. "I'm so happy to discover that we have yet another creative genius in our midst! Well done, young man." She turned to me with a smile. "Now, Miss Myers—what do you have for us today?"

I gulped, glancing down at my project. I'd been so distracted by Logan that instead of making a molecule, I'd glued my toothpicks together into a cube. That's right. A plain, slightly rickety cube. Super creative, right?

"Hmm." The teacher stroked her chin. "Interesting. Please explain your process, my dear?"

"Uh . . ." I shot a helpless look at Gabi and Gwen. They stared back at me, looking curious (Gabi) and amused (Gwen).

Logan interrupted. "I think I can guess what she was thinking. Bailey created this square—"

"Cube," I corrected before I could stop myself.

"This *cube* . . ." He glanced at me, then back at the teacher. "Um, clearly this cube represents the way she sees the world. She's a scientist, you know, and science is all about explaining the world, right? Getting it all to make sense and be logical and stuff. Exploring all the angles." He shrugged. "Angles—like the angles in this cube! Get it?"

"Ah!" Ms. Blumenkranz laughed. "I should have seen it myself. It's creative, yet completely rational—much like Bailey herself. All right, Miss Myers, well done."

Once the teacher had moved on and Gabi and Gwen had

returned to arguing about their casting decisions or whatever, I shot Logan a grateful look. "Thanks," I told him. "I'm not sure I could've talked my way out of that one."

"You're welcome." He grinned, watching as Ms. Blumenkranz exclaimed over a project at another table. "Is she always that— um, you know—enthusiastic?"

"Definitely. So, are you sorry you signed up for art as your elective?" I joked.

"No way—this is cool. At my school in Switzerland, all we did all year in art class was paint the same bowl of fruit. And in California, the teacher was a total bore—he just lectured at us most of the time and hardly let us do anything."

"Wow, you must really like art. It sounds like you've taken it at, like, every school on the planet."

"Just about." He fiddled with his toothpick figure's arms. "Art's just about the only class where I never find out I'm way behind when I start a new school. That's the reason I started signing up for it whenever possible—and I guess somewhere along the way I started to like it."

"I never thought of that," I admitted. "It would be terrible to start a new school and find out I'm half a year behind in biology or something."

"Speaking of biology, what's the teacher like?" He glanced at me. "Mr. Bo or something, right?"

"Mr. Ba," I corrected. "I guess that's a pretty common last name in Senegal, which is where his family emigrated from when he was a kid. He's amazing—super brilliant and a really great teacher. He's working his way through his PhD in evolutionary biology at the university while teaching here full-time."

"Sounds like someone my mom would love." Logan smiled. "Speaking of Mom, she talked me into signing up for the accelerated sophomore bio class, and—"

"You mean fourth period?" I interrupted. "That's the class I'm in!"

Too late, I realized I sounded kind of giddy. Like Taylor whenever she found out her favorite jeans were on sale at the mall. Or Ling whenever she walked into Eats and discovered my great-aunt had just taken a pan of chocolate donuts out of the oven. Or, more recently, Simone when she'd noticed me noticing Logan that first time.

"Really? Awesome!" Logan grinned. "What do you have third period?"

"Gym," I said, trying really hard not to picture him in gym shorts.

"Let me see . . ." Logan pulled out his schedule and consulted it. "No luck, I've got English. What about fifth?"

We went on to compare the rest of our schedules. It turned out that aside from art and bio, the only other class we had in common was a three-days-per-week last-period study hall. I couldn't help feeling disappointed.

"Too bad," Logan said as he tucked his schedule away again. Was it my imagination, or did he actually sound disappointed too? "Maybe I should try to transfer into a few more of your classes." He slid his eyes toward me. "Like I said, it's nice having a friendly face around sometimes."

He reached over to grab the glue, knocking over the bottle in the process. It toppled right onto my toothpick cube, smashing it into a pile of tiny kindling.

"Oh, no! I'm sorry." His face went red, and he reached over as if he was going to try to fix the cube, though it was obviously a lost cause.

"Don't worry about it," I said quickly. "Ms. Blumenkranz already judged it, remember? Besides, if she comes back, I can just tell her that this represents my feelings about the shallowness of modern life."

He laughed, sounding relieved. "Good one."

As he bent to retrieve part of my smashed project that had fallen on the floor, Gabi leaned across the table. "Really hitting it off with the new guy, huh?" she whispered. "Listen, if you get a chance, bat your eyelashes at him and try to convince him to try out for the musical, okay?"

I was so startled that I didn't answer. A moment later Logan was back. "Got it," he said. "Now your angst sculpture is complete."

"Right, yeah." I shot a confused look at Gabi, who was already chattering to Gwen again. What had that been about? Did Gabi really think Logan and I were hitting it off?

That led to the obvious question—could she be onto something? Which led to the corollary question—what if Simone had been right all along? I had to admit, the evidence was starting to mount up. The pounding heart whenever I saw Logan. The light-headed feeling whenever I got close to him. The ability to actually carry on a conversation with him in between panic attacks.

I'd always scoffed at Simone and the others when they'd claimed love at first sight or anything close to it. But now it seemed to be happening to me. I'd never reacted this way to a guy before—*any* guy. I sneaked a peek at Logan, who was bent over his own toothpick sculpture again.

What did it mean? Was I succumbing to teenage hormones at last? Or could there be something different about *this* guy?

Chapter ● Five

When the bell rang, Logan and I walked out of the art room together. We paused in the hall outside as students hurried past in all directions.

I clutched my backpack to my chest. "Well, see you in bio, I guess," I said.

"Yeah." Logan shifted his books to his other arm and glanced around. I expected him to take off, but he just stood there.

"Um, do you know how to get to your next class?" I asked, mostly because I couldn't think of anything else to say.

"Not really." He pulled out his schedule. "It's in the east wing, right? It says the teacher's name is Ms. Wainwright."

Gabi and Gwen emerged from the art room just in time

to hear him. "You've got Wainwright for English next?" Gwen asked Logan. "Me too. I'll take you there."

"Thanks." Logan smiled at her, then glanced at me. "Okay, bye, Bailey."

He reached out and squeezed my shoulder gently. I froze, not sure what he was doing. Maybe he noticed my terrified look, because he instantly yanked his hand back as if it had been burned. Then he ducked his head, his gaze skittering away from mine.

"Yeah, so, see you," he mumbled, turning to follow Gwen, who was already heading down the hall.

"Bye," I said, even though he was probably already too far away to hear me in the crowded hall.

I watched as the shifting sea of humanity swallowed him up. My mind was spinning with crazy thoughts. I was a scientist—I couldn't ignore the evidence anymore. Something unusual was going on here. Yes, I was a bumbling idiot around most guys. But not like *this*. Could I actually be falling for Logan? All the data seemed to support that theory. I'd seen it happen to my friends and others. But what did it mean, exactly? I was glad Simone was in my next class, because I *really* needed to talk to her. I was in way over my head here.

When I stepped into the girls' locker room, the place was already in a full uproar of clanging lockers, talking, and laughter as the female half of the class changed into their gym clothes. I found Simone sitting on the bench in front of our lockers, pulling on her gym socks. Unfortunately, Zoe and a couple of her friends from the softball team were there too. So much for that heart-to-heart I'd hoped to fit in before class. For once I wished Simone wasn't quite so friendly and lovable. It made it hard to get her alone.

Zoe was the first to spot me coming. "Hey, Bailey," she said. "What's up?"

"Nothing," I lied, forcing a smile.

Simone tossed her shoes into her locker, then glanced up at me. "Only one more class to go before I meet my doom," she said with a sigh.

For a second I had no idea what she was talking about. Then I remembered—the bio test. Right.

"You'll be fine," I said, though my heart wasn't in it. I had bigger things on my mind right then than Simone's sloppy study habits.

"That's what I keep telling her." Zoe shrugged. "Anyway, we're sick of hearing about it, Amrou. Time to talk about something else." She sniffed the air. "Like who forgot to take their gym stuff home to wash last week? It reeks in here!"

I sat down on the bench and spun my combination lock as the other girls started playfully accusing one another of stinking up the place. After tossing my books into my locker, I got changed as quickly as I could. Then I just sat there, fiddling with the laces of my sneakers and hoping the others would leave so I could grab a moment with Simone.

No such luck. Simone finished pulling her hair back into a ponytail, slammed her locker shut, and bounced off the bench.

"Let's go!" she said. "I hope we're playing dodgeball or something. I need some distraction."

Zoe clapped me on the back. "Come on, B. You ready?"

"Coming." Swallowing a sigh, I got up and followed Zoe and the others as they followed Simone.

When we emerged into the gym, most of the class was milling around near the locker-room doors. A few of the boys, including Matt and Darius, were kicking a ball around near the bleachers.

"Hey, Ms. Wren's not here yet," Simone said, glancing around the gym. "Quick—quiz me about DNA, Bails, okay?"

Zoe groaned. "Seriously? If you're not ready for that stupid test now, you might as well give it up, Simone."

Simone ignored her, gazing at me with those puppy-dog eyes of hers. "Bails? Pretty please?"

"Sure, okay," I said, still not really thinking about biology. Maybe this was my chance to talk to her about Logan. "Let's go over here where we can have some priv—"

The harsh, high-pitched tweet of a whistle shut me up. The gym teacher strode out of her office and surveyed us as we all turned to look at her.

Ms. Wren's name suited her—she was small and birdlike in her movements, with piercing dark eyes. She taught a couple of remedial freshman math classes as well as gym, and also coached girls' softball and boys' track.

"Listen up, people!" she said. "I've got papers to grade today, so you're doing independent exercise."

"Whoo-hoo!" Matt shouted, pumping his fist in the air.

Ms. Wren fixed her sharp gaze on him. "That does *not* mean goofing off, Matthew. I expect you all to work up a sweat, understand? Hit the weight room, everyone—I'll be watching."

She shooed us toward the weight room adjoining the main part of the gym. Some rich old alumnus had donated a bunch of money a few years earlier, so the place was actually pretty well equipped. There were mats with our school logo on them, a row of free weights along one wall, and all kinds of other exercise machines. Not that I would know good gym equipment from bad, but Zoe claimed it was top of the line.

Once we got inside, Zoe wandered off to stretch or something with the other softball girls, leaving me alone with Simone at last. "Listen . . . ," I began uncertainly.

Simone wasn't paying attention. "Look, Matt and Darius are over by the free weights," she said. "Let's go make fun of their technique, okay?"

"Wait!" I grabbed her arm before she could rush off to join the boys. "Can we just do our own thing for a sec?" I waved at a machine nearby. "I need to talk to you."

"Is it about the test?" Simone looked anxious. "Do you think I'm going to flunk?"

"No. It's just—come on." I dragged her toward the machine.

"Okay, spot me." She sat down and adjusted the weights, then started doing leg lifts. "So what's up, Bails?"

"It's about, um, Logan." I held my breath, hoping she

wouldn't shriek or squeal or anything. At least not too loudly.

"Logan?" She stopped the leg lifts and stared at me, a smile playing around the edges of her mouth. "What about him? I'm right, aren't I? You finally decided you're destined to be together and want me to be the first to know?"

"No. I mean maybe. I mean . . ." I took a deep breath. "Look, I don't know what's going on, okay? That's why I need to talk to you."

She did another leg lift. "Tell me," she said simply.

So I did. I filled her in on everything that had happened in art class, and the confusing thoughts and feelings that had resulted. She listened quietly, her legs steadily pumping up and down.

". . . so then we walked out together, and we were saying good-bye out in the hall before he went to his next class, and things got a little awkward again," I finished. "He kind of squeezed my arm, and then acted like he wished he hadn't, and—"

"Wait—he *touched* you?" Her big brown eyes got even bigger. Dropping the weights, she sat up and spun on the machine's vinyl seat so she was facing me. "Okay, that's major!"

"No, wait, it wasn't a big deal." I immediately guessed by her reaction that I must have overstated what had happened. "I mean, it was just a quick shoulder squeeze. Like this."

I demonstrated on her. She nodded.

"Okay, but it's still him *touching* you. That's key," she said. "I mean, how often do random boys just touch you?"

I thought about that. Not counting adults (like my dad and

uncle) or little kids, or random idiots crashing into me accidentally in the halls because they were horsing around, I couldn't remember the last time a male of the species had made casual skin-to-skin contact. Or skin-to-shirt. Whatever.

Still, I wanted to be logical about this. Study the issue from every angle. Not jump to any conclusions.

"Okay," I said. "But still, Logan has lived all over the world. Maybe he's used to, like, touchier cultures or something."

Simone rolled her eyes. "Oh, please. Why can't you get it through your thick head, Bails? Logan is totally into you! It's obvious you're both—"

"Shh!" I hushed her, noticing that Zoe, Matt, and Darius were coming toward us.

"Hey." Darius flopped down on the rowing machine beside us. "Did I hear you guys talking about Logan?"

"No," I said at the same time Simone said, "Yes."

I shot her a dirty look. She didn't notice, since she was tipping her head up so Matt could give her a quick kiss while Ms. Wren wasn't looking.

"So what're you doing talking about some other guy?" Matt asked Simone in his fake macho voice. "Don't forget, you're *my* woman."

Simone rolled her eyes. "I don't belong to you or anyone else, *man*," she retorted with a smirk. "Anyway, it's not me he's interested in." She slid her eyes in my direction.

"Really?" Zoe looked interested. "Bailey and Logan? Cute."

"No, wait." I didn't want to start this. Not in front of everyone.

Matt leaned against an empty elliptical machine and studied me. "I talked some with Logan in homeroom," he said. "He seems pretty cool. *Maybe* even cool enough to be worthy of going out with Bailey."

"I agree." Simone shot me a smug smile. "You guys need to help me convince her to give him a shot."

Zoe reached over and punched me lightly on the arm. "Go for it, Myers. Logan's hot."

"Hold on, hold on—give the poor girl a break, matchmakers," Darius put in with a laugh. "I mean, she just met the guy. And so what if he's got the hots for her—doesn't mean she has to like him back."

"He doesn't have the hots for me," I blurted out. "I mean, I don't think—I mean . . ." I was totally embarrassed and a little confused. It was becoming an all-too-familiar feeling lately.

"But how does she know if she likes him if she doesn't give him a chance?" Simone argued. "I'm not saying she has to marry the guy or anything."

"Yeah," Matt agreed.

Zoe shrugged. "Hey, Bailey's probably the smartest person I know—she can make up her own mind." She grinned at me. "But for the record, I still say you should go for it."

"Me too," Simone said. "And I know Ling would vote with us if she were here. I was talking to her about Logan last period, and she's already a big fan too."

"Whatever." I could feel that my face was bright red, and it definitely wasn't from pumping iron. "Can we stop talking about this now, please?"

"But—" Simone began.

"Seriously!" I glared at her. "Enough."

Simone shrugged. "Fine."

Matt and Darius traded a look. "Uh, Wren's giving us a dirty look. We should probably get back to it," Darius said.

"Let's hit the power cage next, bro," Matt suggested.

The two guys headed off, with Zoe wandering along behind them. That left me alone with Simone again.

"Um, sorry?" she said, shooting me a sidelong look.

I gritted my teeth. "Does everything have to be a group discussion around here?"

"They just want you to be happy, like I do." Simone got up so I could take her place on the weight machine. "That's why I want you to give Logan a chance. I can tell this guy's different."

"You can?" I asked cautiously.

"I've never seen you react this way to anyone before." Simone gazed at me earnestly as I sat down on the bench and slid my legs under the weight bar. "You've got to see if there's something to this. I'll do whatever I can to help—maybe you guys can double-date with Matt and me if that makes you feel better. Just tell me what you need."

Ms. Wren walked by just then, giving me an excuse not to answer for a moment. I pumped my legs like a madwoman, turning over what Simone was saying in my head. Could she be right? Was it worth trying to find out whether those sparks were real? It was just so hard to believe that someone like me could ever have anything in common with a good-looking, effortlessly popular guy like Logan.

Closing my eyes, I pictured Logan—his adorably crooked smile, his blue eyes, those broad shoulders under his MIT T-shirt . . . Hmm. The MIT shirt reminded me of his science-genius family. Come to think of it, maybe we did have something in common after all.

Hearing a shout of laughter from across the weight room, I opened my eyes and saw Matt and Darius goofing off over there. They were both popular, good-looking guys, and neither of them had seemed weirded out by the idea of me going out with someone like Logan. Neither had Zoe.

So what was the worst that could happen if I gave it a shot? If I decided to follow my heart instead of my head for once, just to see where things might go?

It wasn't such a crazy idea, was it? I mean, even the best scientists had to make a leap of faith once in a while. Otherwise, maybe Darwin never would have come up with his theory of evolution. Alexander Fleming might never have taken a closer look at that mold that became penicillin.

Okay, not that this was the same thing. At all. But maybe that was how I could think of it: as a science experiment.

Like Simone said, what did I have to lose?

Chapter ● Six

How's my hair?" I asked Simone as the two of us headed down the narrow, windowless hallway leading to the science wing. "I hate having gym so early in the day."

She glanced up from her notes, which she was shuffling through frantically as she walked. "Huh? Oh, it's fine. You look gorgeous."

"Thanks." I was actually kind of glad she was so distracted. I was nervous enough about seeing Logan again without Simone giving me flirting advice or trying to put more makeup on me.

When we stepped into Mr. Ba's classroom, more than half the class was there already. Most of them were at their desks, looking pale and anxious as they paged through notes and textbooks, muttering about RNA and nucleotides and stuff.

Simone rushed over to say hi to Taylor and Megan, who were in their seats over near the windows. Taylor had wrapped a strand of blond hair around her pinky finger and was tugging on it, like she always did when she was nervous. Megan looked even paler than usual, and I was pretty sure she was doing a yoga move in her chair to calm herself down.

I lingered just inside the doorway, looking for Logan without quite admitting to myself I was doing it. Mr. Ba's classroom was actually two rooms in one. The front half followed the typical layout with rows of desks. Behind that was the lab, which held a dozen big worktables and all kinds of other equipment. Tall sliding doors could be pulled shut to separate the two areas when necessary (like during dissection weeks, when the smell back there could get a little too strong).

Today the sliding doors were wide open, and there was no sign of Logan in either half of the classroom. What if he'd made a mistake—what if he wasn't in this bio section after all? Maybe he'd changed his schedule since I'd talked to him last, or—

"Bailey! Hey," a voice said directly behind me.

I spun around. "L-Logan!" I blurted out.

"Sorry." He smiled. "Didn't mean to startle you."

"You didn't. I mean, you did. But it's okay. I mean . . ." I forced myself to pause and take a deep breath. So far this wasn't going quite how I'd pictured it. "How was English class?"

"Okay. We're reading *Of Mice and Men*, which I did last year." He stepped aside to let a couple of students hurry into the classroom. "I'm a little more worried about this class, actually. I think it might be more advanced than I realized when I signed up."

"It's not so bad." I shrugged. "I mean, yeah, Mr. Ba can be pretty intense sometimes. But hey, you live with two super-successful scientists, right? Should be a piece of cake for you."

He hesitated, scanning the room. "I don't know. I just—"

"What's going on here?" Mr. Ba's lightly accented voice interrupted him. "You're not thinking of making a run for it before the test starts, Bailey?"

Seeing Mr. Ba always made me smile, and only partly because he taught my favorite subject. He was brilliant and energetic and passionate about science—basically everything I admired and wanted to be someday. He was tall and lean, with skin so dark it was shiny and a wide smile that seemed to swallow up half his face.

"Hi, Mr. Ba," I greeted him. "Nope, not staging an escape. I was just talking to Logan. He's new."

"Yes, so I hear. Welcome, young man." Mr. Ba looked Logan up and down, then pulled a computer printout from the pocket of his corduroy blazer. "Logan Morse, yes?"

"That's right," Logan said. "I hope I'm not too far behind to manage this class."

"Anyone who's willing to open his mind and learn can do just fine here. Come on in." Mr. Ba smiled at Logan, then strode past us into the classroom. "Good morning, class," he said loudly. "We have a new student joining us today—Mr. Morse. He'll be sitting between Mr. Menendez and Ms. Myers. Please adjust yourselves accordingly."

A chorus of groans and complaints rose from the class. "What's going on?" Logan murmured to me.

"Mr. Ba likes alphabetical seating," I whispered back, trying not to grin like a loon when I realized what this meant—I'd be sitting right behind Logan for the rest of the year. "Just one of his little quirks, I guess."

Mr. Ba clapped his hands. "No dilly-dallying! Everyone from Ms. Myers through Ms. Whitman simply move one seat back."

"But the test . . . ," Taylor whined. Her last name was Rhoads, so she was one of the people who needed to move. Since she and Megan had been right across the aisle from each other, it also meant they'd be split up. Too bad for them, but I was sure they'd survive.

"The test shall begin once everyone is in their new seats." Mr. Ba turned toward Logan. "Hmm, now what to do with you?"

"He doesn't have to take the test today, does he?" I asked. Even with Logan's science-savvy DNA, that seemed like too much to ask.

"Of course not," Mr. Ba replied.

"Whew!" Logan blew out a sigh. "That's a relief."

"Take your seat please, Bailey." Mr. Ba gestured for Logan to follow him.

I sat down in my new seat right behind the old one—which was now Logan's. Then I turned and watched as Mr. Ba led Logan through the classroom into the lab area. The teacher's voice carried to the rest of us as he patted the smooth, chemical-resistant top of one of the lab tables.

"Make yourself comfortable, Mr. Morse. Once I get the others started on the test, I'll return and advise you on the reading you'll need to do to catch up. You can take the test in a week or so."

"What?" someone called out. "If he's not even sitting out here today, why'd we have to move seats?"

Mr. Ba ignored the question. He slid the doors shut, blocking Logan from view. "All right, class," he said. "Let's get started."

Once the test paper was in front of me, I forgot about everything else for a while. I was ready for the test. I could have taken it underwater and upside down with one hand tied behind my back. I delved into it, my brain clicking along in overdrive as I filled in the answers.

I was almost disappointed when I finished. Going back over the whole thing, I checked all my answers carefully. Then I looked up. Everyone else was still bent over their papers. Glancing at the clock above the door, I saw that I'd finished early. There were still almost fifteen minutes left in the class period.

After glancing through my answers once more, I stood and walked to the front of the room. "Finished?" Mr. Ba asked, looking up from the book he was reading.

I nodded, dropping my test paper on his desk.

"Show-off," someone muttered from behind me. I was pretty sure it was Taylor. She didn't always deal too well with pressure.

"All right, Bailey, take your seat," Mr. Ba told me. "Or wait, I have a better idea. Why don't you go back and see how Mr. Morse is making out? Perhaps you can help fill him in on the syllabus and answer any questions he might have about the material."

"Oh!" I felt a flutter. "Okay. Sure."

I turned and hurried straight past my desk and all the others. Sliding open the big door just a smidge, I slipped through. Logan was bent over his textbook, but he looked up when he heard the squeak of the door.

"Bailey!" he said. "Hi."

"Hi." I perched on the edge of the other stool at his lab table. "I finished early, so Mr. Ba said I should come back here and hang out." Okay, that wasn't exactly what he'd said. But it was what came out of my mouth. Besides, I doubted Logan actually needed my help getting up to speed in bio. He was practically born and bred to be a whiz in any science class.

"Cool." Logan pushed away the textbook and ran a hand through his hair. "I need a break from this stuff anyway."

"Yeah, I bet it can be tricky trying to figure out exactly where we are compared to your old school."

"It's not just that." Logan sighed and shot me a look. "See, biology isn't really my thing. Every time I try to understand it, my mind just goes all mushy."

"What?" This didn't compute. "But you—I mean . . ." Suddenly I realized what he must be talking about. "Oh, wait. What are you, more of a chemistry guy? Or physics, like your mom?"

"Nope." He shrugged. "I know it's weird, what with my parents and all. But I'm just not really into science." He shot me his lopsided smile. "I think it's really cool that *you're* so into it, though."

That was sweet. But I was too stunned to take it in just then.

He didn't seem to notice my shock. "I guess I just don't have the kind of mind that works that way, you know?" he said. "I'm way better at English, history—that kind of stuff." He shrugged. "I actually do pretty well in those classes. You know—just so you don't think I'm a total idiot."

"I don't think that," I said quickly.

My mind was spinning. Ever since I'd heard about his parents, I'd assumed he was like me, at least in that one very important way. That science was what the two of us had in common. That our common interests might possibly be the source of those sparks. A meeting of the minds or something.

Now? I wasn't sure *what* to think.

Before I could figure it out, the sliding door slid open a bit. I looked up, expecting it to be Mr. Ba. Instead, I was surprised to see Megan slipping her curvy form through the small opening.

"What happened?" I blurted out. "Did you give up?"

Megan laughed, tossing her head so her luscious red waves danced around her shoulders. "Don't be silly, Bailey. I finished early, just like you."

"You—you did?" That was a first. Megan wasn't normally a star student in bio. Far from it, actually.

But I wasn't too worried about Megan's newfound science smarts. I was still focused on Logan's confession. This changed everything. Didn't it?

Megan slid a stool over to join us. The lab tables were meant for two people, so we all ended up sort of squished together, with Logan in the middle.

"So how's it going?" Megan asked him. "Is Bailey helping you get caught up? She's, like, the smartest person in the class, so you can trust what she tells you."

"Yeah, she's been great." Logan flashed me a smile.

Megan leaned on the table, chin in her hand and green eyes focused on Logan. "So Ling tells me you've lived all over the world, Logan."

"Yeah, she was asking me about that in English class," he said.

"Oh, right." I suddenly remembered that Ling had English third period. "I forgot she'd be in your class. I would've told you to look for her."

"She found me," Logan said. "She's really friendly."

"Yeah, she's cool." Megan played with the ends of her hair. "So what's it like to live overseas? We're always fantasizing about traveling through Europe, right, Bailey?"

"Um, yeah?" I vaguely recalled Megan and Simone giggling about fantasy shopping trips to Paris or Milan a few times.

"I don't know, it actually seems pretty normal to me at this point." Logan shrugged. "Makes it kind of complicated to transfer to a school here, though. I'm supposed to have yet another meeting with the guidance counselor right after this."

Megan wrinkled her nose, a move that made most people look like a ferret but only accentuated her perfect features. "But it's lunch period next. Mr. Vance isn't making you meet with him during lunch, is he? That's cruel and unusual."

Logan chuckled. "He said it would probably only take a few minutes, so I probably won't starve to death."

"That's good." Megan touched him lightly on the back of one hand. "And listen, when you get to the caf, you should come sit with us. Right, Bailey?"

"Sure." I was starting to feel uncomfortable. Had Simone told Megan I might be interested in Logan? Because she seemed to be going out of her way to get him to our lunch table. "I mean, if you want to," I added.

"Sounds good," Logan said.

"Great." Megan flashed him her megawatt smile. "Our table's over near the windows. My personal philosophy is that no new kid should have to eat alone on his first day."

That definitely *wasn't* her personal philosophy. Megan had never been much of a welcome-wagon type before. Which made me more certain than ever that this was all part of Simone's master plan to get me together with Logan. I was a little annoyed that she was still involving our friends in her sneaky plans, especially after that embarrassing group discussion in gym.

I slid my gaze toward Logan, hoping he hadn't caught on to

what Megan was doing. He wasn't looking at either of us. His eyes were on the bio textbook still open in front of him. A worried little frown creased his forehead, making him look adorably vulnerable.

Okay. So maybe I wasn't really *that* annoyed.

Chapter Seven

By the time I grabbed my bagged lunch from my locker and reached the cafeteria, Simone, Zoe, Megan, and Taylor were already seated at our usual table. Taylor and Simone were still moaning about the bio quiz, while Megan and Zoe were debating whether to try to hit some sale going on at the mall.

"Where are the guys?" I asked as I took my seat. Lately Matt and Darius had been sitting with us nearly every day.

Simone looked up from unwrapping her sandwich. "They're eating in the auditorium today. The lacrosse team has a fundraiser meeting or something."

"Oh." I was relieved to hear it. That conversation with Megan and Logan after the bio test had made me realize I needed to talk to my friends about the whole Logan situation. In fact, it would be stupid *not* to talk to them. Unlike me, the five of them had tons of experience with guys and dating. Practically every guy in school had been after Megan since they'd stopped thinking girls had cooties. Zoe had actually been the first of our group to kiss a guy, way back in fifth grade—specifically this kid from another school she met during a track meet—and she'd gone out with a couple of other guys since. Taylor and Ling regularly had multiple guys drooling over them. And of course Simone was pretty much the queen of romance.

And that was all good. Because I was going to need a whole team behind me if I was to have any hope of figuring this thing out. Besides, I might as well discuss it with them myself, since it was pretty obvious Simone must have filled Megan in already. Or maybe Zoe had told Megan, since she definitely knew something was going on thanks to that awkward conversation in gym class. Either way, if the rest of them knew, Taylor and Ling were likely to know soon if they didn't already.

Speaking of Ling, she hadn't shown up yet. I glanced over at the lunch line, trying to spot her. No sense getting into it before we were all there.

Then again, I couldn't resist feeling the others out a little. "So, too bad the guys aren't going to be here today." I kept my voice casual and my eyes on my bag as I unpacked my food. "Megan invited Logan to sit with us, and he might not expect to be the only guy."

"Yeah, Logan and I had a nice little chat during bio." Megan selected a pretzel from the bag in front of her, holding it up and examining it from all angles. "I'm sure you've all noticed how hot he is, right?"

"Uh-huh." Simone smirked at me and waggled her eyebrows. "Some of us have *definitely* noticed."

Megan shot her a suspicious look. "Well, don't get too excited," she said. "I'm calling dibs on him."

"What?" Simone blurted out, She spun and looked at me again. "But—"

I kicked her under the table. Hard. My heart was pounding and I felt a little sick. Was this really happening? Had Megan really just called dibs on Logan like he was the last cupcake on the platter?

"Yeah, I know he's not my usual type," Megan said. "But he's super smart and cool and really, really sweet, right? I could get used to that for sure."

Well, that was it, then. Megan was the hottest girl in school. No way could I compete with that. I avoided Simone's eyes as she turned to stare at me.

Meanwhile Taylor and Zoe had barely looked up from their food at Megan's announcement. "Whatever," Taylor said. "He's not my type either."

Zoe shot me a curious look, but I kept my gaze on my lunch. "Yeah, I guess he's all yours, Megan." Zoe raised her iced tea in salute. "Good luck. You guys will make a cute couple."

Simone was frowning. "Look, Megan. Logan is his own person. You can't just call dibs on a *person*."

"Yes, I can." Megan calmly popped a pretzel into her mouth. "I just did."

At that moment, Ling finally arrived. "Hey," she greeted us, sliding her lunch tray into the empty spot beside Zoe. "What's with the face, Simone? Did you flunk your test?"

"Big news," Taylor said. "Megan just called dibs on the new guy, Logan."

"*What?*" Ling's head snapped up and her eyes trained on Megan like laser beams. "No way."

"Yes way." Megan licked salt off her fingers, looking smug. "We totally bonded during bio last period."

Ling glared at her. "Well, that's too bad," she said icily. "Because Logan and *I* totally bonded during English the period before that. Which means if anyone gets dibs on him, it's me."

Megan frowned. "That's not how it works—I already called it. You snooze, you lose."

"She's got you there, Ling," Zoe put in with a laugh.

"Shut up." Ling shot her a poisonous look, then turned her evil eye back on Megan. "You can't call dibs on a guy. That's stupid."

"Yeah, that's what Simone said," Taylor put in.

"Who asked you?" Megan snapped.

I sneaked a peek at Simone. She looked annoyed and frustrated. When she caught me looking, she widened her eyes at me. I tightened my lips and shook my head, willing her not to blurt out anything stupid.

"Calling dibs on Logan is completely ridiculous," Simone

said. "If more than one person is interested in him, it makes just as much sense to draw straws."

"Why?" Megan challenged her. "Because you moved too slow to call him for yourself?"

Simone blew out a loud sigh of frustration. "I'm not saying I want him for myself!" she exclaimed. "I'm just saying—"

"Simone—listen," I interrupted, yanking her arm so hard she had to grab the edge of the table to keep her balance. "Have you seen my phone? I think I left it in your locker."

"What?" She glanced at me with a frown. "You didn't put it—"

"Yes, I did. Remember?" This time I was the one widening my eyes in a meaningful way.

Fortunately, she caught on. "Oh, right. Um, come on, we'd better check."

The others barely noticed as we slipped away. Megan and Ling were still facing off, with Zoe and Taylor egging them on.

As soon as Simone and I reached a private spot in the hall outside the cafeteria, I turned to face her. "Don't," I said. "It's okay."

"No, it's not!" She put her hands on her hips. "So what if those two have suddenly decided they want Logan? It doesn't change the fact that this is the first guy who's ever made you go all gooey. It doesn't change the way he feels about you, either."

"It might," I said, thinking of Megan's overwhelming radiance, Ling's cool beauty.

She gave me a little shove. "Stop. You know you like him. It's obvious to anyone with eyes and a heart. So why not give it a go?"

"Were you there just now?" I shook my head. "Megan and Ling both want him. I've got no chance."

"You don't know that," she said. "So you might as well give it a try and see what happens. Megan and Ling aren't the type to hold grudges over guy stuff." She hesitated. "Probably not, anyway."

I rolled my eyes. "Forget it. It's just not worth the angst." I held up one hand like a witness swearing in on some court-room drama. "I hereby officially withdraw my interest in one Mr. Logan Morse."

"Stop." Simone slapped my hand down. "You don't have to—"

"I *want* to," I said firmly. "Seriously. It's kind of a relief, really. Now I can stick to my life plan, do my thing. Whew!" I mimed wiping sweat from my brow.

She had a little frown on her face as she held my eye. "Are you sure about this?"

"Positive." I crossed my heart. "It's over, okay?"

"Do you want to talk about it?"

"No." I avoided her eye. "Not right now, anyway. Maybe later."

That seemed to satisfy her, though she still seemed unsettled. "Fine," she said. "Let's get back in there before Zoe eats all my chips."

We headed into the cafeteria. As we neared our table, I could see that Megan had a big smile on her face. Across from her, Ling looked serene as she sipped her soda. Was the fight over already? If so, who had won?

Then I saw Logan winding his way between tables, heading toward my friends. Ah, that explained it. Megan and Ling weren't about to let him see them fighting over him. If I knew them—and I did—they wouldn't want him to catch even the slightest whiff of pettiness or desperation or less than full control.

I slid into my seat moments before Logan reached the table. "Find your phone?" Zoe asked.

"What?" I said. "Oh, right, yeah." I patted my backpack, where my phone had been all along.

Then I watched out of the corner of my eye as Logan arrived. "Hi, everyone," he said. "Bailey and Megan said I could sit with you guys today?"

He made a move toward the empty seat beside me. Ling jumped out of her chair, quick as a wink.

"Come sit over here, Logan," she said, patting the chair she'd just vacated as she slid into the empty one right next to it. "You'll be able to see the entire room from here. I can point out everyone important."

"Great idea." Megan slid her chair around the corner of the table so it was beside the one Ling had indicated for Logan. "I can help point out who's cool and who you should avoid."

She put a tiny bit of emphasis on the last word, glaring at Ling behind Logan's back. Zoe started to laugh, but covered it by pretending to cough. Taylor just rolled her eyes and ate another cookie.

"Um, okay." Logan shot me a slightly confused look, but allowed Ling and Megan to herd him into his new seat.

For the next few minutes Simone, Zoe, Taylor, and I were treated to a master's seminar on flirting techniques. Finally, when Megan tossed her long red hair for about the fifteenth time, I'd had enough. Quickly cramming my last few carrot sticks into my mouth, I crumpled my empty bag and stood up.

"See you later," I said to the table at large, carefully avoiding meeting anyone's eye. Especially Logan's or Simone's. "I need to go to the library. I want to, uh, start researching my social-studies project."

I hurried away without waiting for an answer.

Chapter ● Eight

The rest of the day passed slowly. I wandered from class to class, trying to focus on the teachers and put Logan out of my mind.

That wasn't as easy as expected. He kept popping into my head at odd moments. When I walked past the bulletin board near the art room and noticed an anime-inspired project hanging there, I thought about Logan living in Tokyo. When one of my teachers mentioned dinosaurs, my mind jumped straight to Logan's dad's job and his new book. And every time I was in the halls between classes, I caught myself looking for Logan in the crowd. Every. Time.

What was that about? I was a practical person. I knew it was pointless to waste time and brain cells mooning over something that was never going to happen.

Still, as last period approached, things seemed to be getting worse instead of better. I caught myself counting down the minutes until study hall. When the bell rang to end English class, I wanted to leap up from my seat and race out of the room. Instead I forced myself to stand up calmly, collect my books, and stroll out. Then I meandered down the hall in a most leisurely manner, even stopping along the way to examine the sign-up sheet and poster hanging on the wall outside the drama room.

As I stood there, Gwen emerged from the room. "Oh, hi, Bailey," she said, tugging at the hem of her black sweater. "Hey, did you convince your studly new friend to try out for Lancelot yet?"

"What? I mean no." I willed myself not to blush. "Sorry. I, uh, haven't really talked to him much since art class."

"Oh, well." She shrugged. "Better get a move on—second bell's about to ring."

Oh, crap, she was right. A glance at my watch showed that I was about to be late. Okay, so Mr. Gillespie wasn't very strict about arriving on time to his study halls. He wasn't very strict about anything, actually. That didn't mean I wanted to risk getting caught out in the halls by the vice principal or one of the teachers who actually cared about punctuality.

Luckily, Gillespie's room was close by. I raced around the corner and hurtled toward the door. My momentum was such that I almost didn't notice someone standing in the doorway.

"Logan!" I blurted out, skidding to a stop just in time to avoid crashing into him. I swallowed hard as I saw Ling standing beside him. In fact, she was standing so close that her long hair was brushing his arm. "Um, hi, Ling," I added. "What are you doing here?"

"I was just walking Logan to study hall." Ling leaned even closer and grabbed his arm, tilting her head up and smiling at him. "We wouldn't want him to get lost, right?"

"Definitely not," I muttered, starting to move around them.

Logan reached out and stopped me. "That's right, you're in this study hall too, aren't you?" he said brightly.

My arm tingled where he'd just touched it. Then I realized what he'd just said. Had he really forgotten we had this study hall together? Obviously the intersections in our schedule, few as they were, hadn't made the same kind of impression on him as they had on me.

"That's right," I said, forcing a tight smile. "Monday, Wednesday, and Friday."

"Cool." Logan glanced at Ling. "Well, thanks for showing me the way. I should get in there. Hope I didn't make you late for your next class."

Ling checked her watch. "Yeah, guess I'd better get going. Later, Logan. See you, Bailey."

"Bye," I muttered.

"After you." Logan swept an arm out to let me walk in first. I nodded, then ducked my head and hurried inside.

Simone and Taylor were in their usual seats near the back,

huddled over a magazine. I headed toward them, expecting Logan to peel off and do his own thing. I was a little surprised when I realized he was following me.

Then again, why wouldn't he? My friends and I were probably the only people he knew in this class. It was only natural he would cling to us until he got his bearings at his new school. Sort of like an animal trying to fit in with a new pack or herd.

Simone's eyes brightened when she saw us coming. I glared at her, trying to head off any embarrassing comments.

"Hi, Logan!" Simone's voice sounded as cheerful and fake as a bad actor in an infomercial. "I didn't know you were in this study hall."

Liar. I'd told her that during gym.

"Yeah." Logan gestured toward several empty desks nearby. "So are there assigned seats here, or what?"

"Nope." Taylor flipped another page in her magazine. "Gillespie doesn't care what we do as long as we keep it down to a dull roar."

"Cool." Logan glanced at me. "Where do you usually sit, Bailey? I don't want to steal your seat."

I dropped my bag on my usual desk in front of Simone. "Right here?" It came out sounding more like a question than an answer.

"Okay." Logan sat down at the desk next to mine. "Then I guess I'll sit here. So the teacher doesn't mind if we talk?"

"Not at all." Simone glanced at Mr. Gillespie, who was at the front of the room chatting with several members of the JV baseball team, which he coached. "We could probably throw a party and he wouldn't care."

"Yeah." Taylor was sitting behind Logan. She leaned forward. "So how's your first day going?"

"Not too bad." Logan shrugged. "Everyone here seems pretty cool so far."

Taylor laughed. "That's because you don't know them that well yet," she joked.

Simone leaned across the aisle and grabbed the magazine out of Taylor's hands. "Hey, we've already looked at this one a zillion times," she said, jumping to her feet. "Let's go over and ask Maria if she has anything new we can borrow."

"Hey! What?" Taylor complained. "I just bought that yester—*ow!* Quit it!"

Simone quickly pulled her hand back, leaving Taylor rubbing her arm where Simone had pinched it. "Come on." Simone raised her eyebrows at Taylor. "Let's *go*."

"Whatever." Looking confused, Taylor hauled herself out of her seat and allowed Simone to hustle her off across the room.

I winced, hoping Logan hadn't caught any of that. Subtle was definitely not Simone's middle name.

When I looked over, Logan was digging into the outside pocket of his backpack. He pulled out a pack of mints.

"Want one?" he asked, holding it out. "I don't know about you, but I need a little sugar rush this time of day."

"Thanks." I took a mint, being careful not to let my fingers touch his. I didn't need that embarrassing tingling to start up again.

He popped a mint, then tossed the pack back in his bag. I sucked on my mint, hoping the sharp spearmint might clear my mind. I couldn't believe Simone was still trying to push me and Logan together after what had happened at lunch. Was she nuts?

Then again, why did I expect any different? I already knew Simone wasn't exactly logical when it came to romance. Or anything else, for that matter.

However, *I* still retained the capacity for logical thought even if my best friend didn't. And when I thought about it logically, I realized there might be a silver lining to Simone's nuttiness. So what if she'd arranged things so I was stuck talking to Logan for a while? He was a nice guy, and even if that whole sparks thing was a nonstarter, there was no reason he and I couldn't be friends. In fact, if he was going to end up going out with either Megan or Ling, it would be better if we had at least a cordial relationship, right? Plus, bonus: He was much easier to talk to than most guys. Chatting with him would be good practice for me so I didn't end up completely tongue-tied if and when I *did* meet Mr. Right in college or whenever.

Before I could think of a way to launch a friendly conversation, Logan did it for me. "Ling tells me you and Simone have been friends for a long time," he said.

"Our whole lives," I said. "Our moms are friends, and they had us doing playdates together from the time we could sit up, if not before. Although based on their stories, it sounds like the playdates were mostly an excuse for them to get together and drink wine in the afternoon."

Logan laughed. "Sounds sort of like my dad and his friends. Mom seems suspicious that most of their so-called work conferences take place in the vicinity of good pubs or famous golf courses."

"You said your dad's a paleontologist, right? That must be a really interesting job."

"He loves it. Especially loves getting his hands dirty digging around for old bones or whatever." Logan drummed his fingers on his desk. "I'm kind of glad he decided to write this book, though. Back when I was a little kid, before Mom decided to go back for her PhD, Dad used to have to travel a ton. It seemed like he was away on digs more than he was home. We had to move a lot just to stay in the same hemisphere as him."

"Really?" I shook my head. "I can't imagine what it's like to move as much as you have. Like I told you, I've never lived anywhere but here." I glanced around the room. I'd known most of the people there since kindergarten.

"I guess I'm just used to being a nomad." He glanced around too. "Actually, it's hard for me to imagine that this might be it for a while—that I might be at this school all the way through graduation." He bit his lip. "It weirds me out a little bit, to be honest."

I wasn't sure how to respond for a moment. His blue eyes had taken on a faraway expression, and his lips were tilted in a little half frown. Suddenly this didn't feel so much like a casual, friendly conversation anymore. . . .

"Um, graduation's only a little over two years away," I said. "That's not very long."

"I guess. Although Mom's already talking about me going to the university here too—I'd get free tuition since she's on the faculty." He rolled his eyes. "Luckily, Dad already told me I can go anywhere I want."

"Where do you want to go?" I asked.

He lifted one shoulder. "Haven't thought about it that much. Maybe I'll go back abroad—it might be fun to study in Europe. Or maybe South America. I've never lived there, but we all went to Peru once when Dad had a conference in Trujillo."

I shook my head, amazed by how casually he talked about stuff like that. "Wow. I never really thought about going to college in another country. I'm worried enough about how I'm going to handle living in another *state*!"

"You'll do fine." Logan smiled. "You'll fit right in at MIT."

"*If* I get in," I said quickly. "And *if* I can figure out a way to pay for it. My family does okay, but they're not going to be able to pay that kind of tuition by selling a few more of Great-Aunt Ellen's chocolate-chip cookies."

He shrugged. "You can get loans, right?"

"Maybe for part of it." I stared across the room at Mr. Gillespie, who was kicking a half-deflated soccer ball around with a couple of the baseball guys. But I wasn't really seeing them. No, I was looking at my future. My sad, pathetic future stuck working for-ever at Eats if I didn't get the scholarships I needed. "But I can't afford to run up too much debt in undergrad," I told Logan. "Not with med school coming up right afterward."

"Med school? You want to be a doctor?"

"Medical researcher," I said. "I want to study genetics. Or maybe cellular biology or something along those lines. I haven't quite decided yet, but I figure I can try a few different things in college and narrow it down by the time I get through med school."

"Wow." He looked impressed. "You've really put a lot of thought into this."

"I know, everyone thinks I'm a freak." I shot a look at Simone and Taylor, who were still hanging out near the front of the room. "Most of my friends haven't even started thinking about college yet."

"You're not a freak for thinking ahead." He leaned across the aisle, gazing at me intently. "It's cool that you know what you want. Most people our age don't."

Okay, that definitely wasn't the usual response I got when I started spouting off about college plans. Simone usually just sighed and rolled her eyes. The other girls mostly ignored me and changed the subject. And the one time I'd mentioned watch-ing an Internet video of a college-level genetics class, Matt and Darius had looked at me as if I was some weirdo from the planet Intellecto, and Matt had nicknamed me Professor for a day or two until he forgot about it.

But here was Logan, looking at me as if this was a perfectly normal—even admirable—topic for a high school sophomore to discuss. That was different. *He* was different.

Uh-oh. All of a sudden that sparky, fluttery feeling was back again, stronger than ever.

"Anyway, enough about me." I forced a laugh, ready to steer things back to more comfortable ground. "How's your new house? Are you all moved in?"

"Pretty much." He brightened. "And hey, that reminds me—there's at least one good thing about being stuck in one place for a while."

"What's that?"

"I've always wanted a dog, but we moved around way too much before." He grinned like a little kid. "Now that we're here, Mom and Dad said I can finally get one!"

"That's cool. What kind of dog are you going to get?"

"I'm not sure yet. Do you have any pets?" he asked. "I could use some advice."

"We just have a cat right now," I said. "Our old dog died last year. He was a beagle."

"That's one of the breeds on my list," Logan said. "Along with retrievers and a few others. But I'll probably just end up going to the pound and picking out a lovable mutt."

"Sounds good." I could totally picture him with a dog. Then I thought of something. "But wait, what if you do end up going to college abroad? Will you be able to take the dog with you?"

He shrugged. "I don't know. Maybe. If not, it could stay here with my parents. I think Dad's almost as excited about the dog thing as I am."

"That's cool." I smiled, but I was feeling kind of confused. One minute Logan was talking about getting settled in and living here forever. The next it seemed like he already had one foot on the plane back to Europe or wherever.

Not that there was anything wrong with that. I had no intention of getting stuck in this town forever myself. But it reminded me that high school wouldn't last forever, even if it felt that way sometimes. The two-plus years we had left were practically nothing, especially if you looked at time in geologic terms. After graduation we were all likely to go off in different directions. So even if Ling and Megan weren't in the picture, what was the point in getting involved with a guy now?

And of course Ling and Megan *were* in the picture. They were both used to getting what they wanted, and they weren't going to back off just because I had some kind of wishy-washy flutter in my gut over this particular guy.

So that was two pretty big strikes against even considering being more than friends with Logan. The logical part of my mind said not to bother.

So why did I keep feeling those sparks?

Chapter • Nine

College Avenue Eats was almost deserted when I arrived after school. Two older ladies were chatting over coffee and pastries, and a harried-looking college student was typing away madly on her laptop, a half-eaten bowl of soup cooling beside her. My uncle was over by the counter spritzing glass cleaner on the display cases, while my mother was pulling several dozen snicker-doodles off a tray and putting them into a basket in the bakery case.

"Yum," I said, hurrying over and grabbing a cookie before she could add it to the display. "Did Great-Aunt Ellen just make these?"

"Uh-huh. And don't eat any more—you know she only works a half day on Mondays, and we're likely to run out before dinnertime as it is." Mom slapped my hand away before I could take more. "How was school? Did your biology test go okay?"

"Test was good. School was fine." I stuffed the cookie in my mouth. It was still warm—heaven. Great-Aunt Ellen was the one who'd first convinced my great-grandparents to add a bakery to their successful deli business way back in the early days. It had been a hit from the start, probably because her cookies, cakes, and donuts were so delicious that people came from miles around to get them.

I wiped my hand on my jeans, then went behind the counter and grabbed one of the coffee pots from the twin burners. The two older ladies were regular customers, and I knew they always drank decaf.

"Refill?" I asked when I reached their table.

"Oh, thank you, dear." The older of the pair smiled at me and slid her cup closer.

"Yes, thanks." Her friend pushed her glasses up her nose and peered toward the bakery case. "Did I just see your mother bringing out some fresh cookies?"

"Snickerdoodles." I smiled. "How many do you want?"

Once I'd finished topping off their coffee and brought them each a cookie, I stepped behind the counter and put the coffee pot back. "What do you want me to do?" I asked.

Uncle Rick glanced up from his cleaning. "Suz is in back working on a delivery order," he said. "You could help her finish up."

"Okay." I pushed through the swinging doors.

Susannah glanced up from layering ham and provolone onto a row of sub rolls. "Hi, Bailey."

"Hi. How'd your test go?"

She groaned. "Don't ask. How was yours?"

"The usual." I shrugged. "Simone thinks she actually passed, though."

"That's good." She shoved a tub of mayonnaise toward me. "Here. I need two roast beef with lettuce, onion, and mayo. No tomato."

"Got it."

We worked together in comfortable silence. When the sandwiches were finished, Susannah started stuffing them into bags. "Can you tell your dad these are ready?" she said. "He's in the office."

I nodded and stepped into the tiny hallway beyond the kitchen. Passing the storerooms and restroom, I stopped in front of the closetlike office. Through the half-open door I could see my dad at the desk, bent over some paperwork. I rapped lightly on the door frame.

"Order's up," I said.

Dad looked up, his mustache twitching into a smile. "Oh, hi, Bailey. I didn't know you were here. What time is it?" He checked his watch.

"Time to deliver some sandwiches. Do you want me to take them? Or ask Uncle Rick?"

"No, I've got it." Dad stood and stretched. "I can swing by

and pick your sister up from her piano lesson on the way back."

I followed him out to the front. Things were still slow, so Mom suggested I get started on my homework. I took her advice, slipping into the corner booth and pulling out my books.

I was halfway through that night's geometry proofs when the bell over the door jingled loudly. Once I looked up, I saw that it was Megan. She'd changed out of her school clothes into a pretty floral wrap dress with a deep V-neck. It definitely hugged her curves in all the right places, though the cap sleeves and light-weight, flowy fabric looked more suited for July than the fickle weather of early spring.

"Bailey! I was hoping you'd be here!" She hurried over and slid onto the bench across from me. Her eyes were dancing with excitement and her cheeks were flushed pink. The latter was probably due to vasodilation from spending time outdoors in that dress on a relatively chilly day. But somehow, since she was Megan, it only made her look more beautiful than ever.

I lowered my pencil. "I'm always here," I joked, trying not to stare at her cleavage. "You know that."

"Yeah." She dug into her purse and pulled out a jeweled compact, checking her face and hair in the tiny mirror. "So how about that scene at lunch today? Is Ling a nut, or what?"

"Hmm." I wasn't about to start taking sides between the two of them. That would only make an already ridiculous situation downright insane.

"I mean, I can't believe she's trying to steal Logan right out from under me!" Megan snapped her compact shut and tucked it back into her purse. "He's so not her type."

"I guess." She actually had a point there. Ling had an edge to her, and she usually preferred a guy who could stand up to her—even challenge her. Obviously I didn't know Logan that well yet, but he seemed too easygoing to fill that role.

Then again, Megan herself had pointed out that Logan wasn't really *her* usual type either. Okay, yes, he was good-looking and fit. But not exactly the dumb-jock kind of guy she usually preferred.

Megan ran her fingers through her glossy red hair, which as usual looked ready for that shampoo ad. "I guess I can't blame her, though," she said. "I mean, Logan is pretty amazing, right? It's about time we got some cool new guys around here."

I nodded, gripping my pencil tightly. Why was she telling me this? All my friends knew I wasn't exactly the go-to girl for romantic advice. Why wasn't Megan spilling her guts to Taylor or Zoe or Simone? Why me?

"Anyway, I'm sure Ling will come to her senses soon. At least I hope so." Megan leaned forward. "In the meantime, I had a wonderful idea."

"Really?" I asked weakly. Couldn't she see that I didn't want to have this conversation?

No, probably not, I realized immediately. Megan was a great friend in most ways. She was loyal, fun-loving, and quick to laugh. But she could be single-minded when she was involved in something, and occasionally maybe a little slow to notice what other people might be feeling.

"I want to do something special for Logan," she said eagerly. "You know, like, to welcome him to town? So I want to commission a special cupcake for him."

"A cupcake?" That wasn't what I was expecting.

"Right. And you're the expert at this stuff, Bailey. How many words can I fit on one cupcake? Can I make it say 'Welcome Logan, from Megan?' Or maybe something longer?"

"I don't really do much with the bakery stuff," I told her. "And my great-aunt already left for the day. Maybe it could wait until tomorrow?"

"No!" Her eyes widened. "I want to deliver it to his house today. Can't you make me one?"

"Trust me, you don't want to give anything I've baked to anyone you like," I said. She looked so distraught that I relented. "But maybe Susannah could write something on an already-made cupcake. . . ."

"Perfect!" Megan clapped her hands. "Come on, help me explain it to her."

Susannah was in the back prepping for the dinner rush. She nodded when she heard what we wanted. "We're sold out of chocolate already. White cupcake okay?" she asked.

"Fine, whatever." Megan didn't seem too interested in the details. "How long will it take you to do the writing?"

"I need to finish this first." Susannah nodded at the half-chopped head of iceberg in front of her. "So maybe half an hour?"

"Great. I'll be back then to pick it up." Megan grabbed me in a quick hug, enveloping me in her signature jasmine cologne. "Thanks, guys!"

After she rushed out, I slumped against the counter and stared into space. For a while there during study hall, I'd almost started to wonder if maybe Simone was right. If it really was worth taking a chance on this sparks thing.

But this? This had brought me back to earth.

"Bailey?" Susannah said. "What's the matter? You look down."

I blinked, remembering where I was. "What? No, I'm fine."

"Bailey. It's me." My cousin lowered her knife again and watched me. "This new guy your friend was talking about—her cupcake boy. It's not the cute boy who came in yesterday, is it? The one Simone said you were hitting it off with?"

"Simone told you that?" I gritted my teeth. "That girl has *such* a big mouth!"

"You're just figuring this out now?" Susannah smiled. "But seriously, what's the deal?"

My first instinct was to brush her off, find an excuse to change the subject or go back out front. Then again, maybe I shouldn't be so hasty. Susannah was both a natural romantic and a realist. She'd gone out with all kinds of guys throughout high school, from bad boys to jocks to nerds and everything in between. But the only one who'd stuck for more than a couple of months was her current boyfriend, Chuck, a fellow business student who was already expressing an interest in joining the family business some-day. Practical, right? She'd played the field but settled on a guy who fit in perfectly with her life plan. Maybe hers was exactly the kind of advice I needed right now.

She was still watching me as she went back to chopping. "Bailey? Come on, you know you can trust me."

"I know." I glanced around to make sure we were alone. Mom and Uncle Rick were out front, Dad was still out making that delivery. Susannah's mom, Aunt Vera, was off today, and the extra evening staff hadn't arrived yet. "The thing is, I'm not exactly sure what the deal is myself. There's something different about Logan."

"Logan. I like his name." Susannah nodded, scooping the chopped lettuce into a bowl with the edge of her knife. "What's different about him?"

"I don't know!" I wailed. "That's the trouble. It's like as soon as he walked in, I felt like I already knew him. No, wait." I stopped and thought about that. "That's not really true. But I *wanted* to know him. Or something . . . Aargh!" I clutched my hair.

"Wow." Susannah sliced through another head of lettuce, then paused and looked at me. "That definitely doesn't sound like you. Tell me more."

"So we've talked a few times since then, and it just keeps getting weirder. I like talking to him, and sometimes it feels almost like talking to a friend, even though we don't know each other that well and, you know, he's a guy. But sometimes I get all nervous and freaked out, and I can't think of anything to say that won't sound totally idiotic." I grimaced. "Simone calls it sparks."

"Okay." Susannah went back to work, her knife efficiently slicing the lettuce into strips. "And do the sparks go both ways? Does he feel the same about you?"

I frowned at her. "How should I know? I'm not a mind reader."

She laughed. "I forgot who I'm talking to," she said. "I just mean, does he seem to like talking to you? Does he look you in the eye when you're together? Does he ever, like, touch you on the hand or anything like that?"

"I guess. Maybe. Sort of. But it doesn't matter. See, Megan and Ling both called dibs on him."

"Dibs?" Susannah's knife paused in midslice, and she blinked at me. "What are you talking about?"

I told her about the scene in the cafeteria. "So even if I'm not imagining what I'm feeling, it doesn't matter," I finished with a sigh. "He's already spoken for."

"Not necessarily." Susannah scraped another pile of chopped lettuce off the cutting board and dumped it into the bowl. "It takes two to tango."

"Huh?"

She grabbed a rag and wiped her hands. "If the sparks are mutual, Logan isn't going to be interested in your friends no matter how much they throw themselves at him. Or how pretty they are. Or how many customized cupcakes they give him. Which reminds me—wait here."

She hurried out through the swinging doors. I grabbed a

rag and started wiping down the area where she'd been working, hoping the mindless task would settle me down.

Susannah reappeared a moment later with a cupcake. She set it on the marble counter over in the bakery area, then started digging through a cabinet.

"Did your mom move the frosting tips again?" she said. "No, wait—here they are."

I wandered over to watch as she fitted a tip to a fresh pastry bag. "Do you really think there's any chance he wouldn't be interested in Megan or Ling?" I asked. "Even though every other guy in school would kill to go out with them?"

"Of course. If he likes you, he likes *you*. He won't settle for some other girl."

"But how do I know if he likes me?" I couldn't believe this was me asking that. "Or even if I actually like him? I mean, we hardly know each other!"

Susannah leaned over the cupcake, carefully forming letters with the frosting in her bag. "Spend more time with him. Get to know each other better. Then you'll know."

"How? We only have three classes together."

"You could ask him out."

"What?" I squawked at the top of my lungs.

"Easy, girl!" She glanced up from her task. "As a *friend*. You could start by hanging out as friends. He's new in town, so it's only natural that you'd want to help show him around, right? Just invite him to do something casual."

That actually didn't sound so bad. "Like what?"

She shrugged. "The Spring Thing's coming up. You could ask him to come cheer you on at the kickball tournament."

"Right. Come watch me get sweaty and covered in mud," I muttered. "Very romantic."

She laughed. "Okay, you have a point. Besides, that's still a week and a half away. But I'm sure you can come up with something."

Just then Uncle Rick stuck his head into the kitchen. "Bailey, up front," he said. "Someone's here to see you."

He ducked out of sight again. I glanced at the cupcake, which was only half inscribed.

"That's got to be Megan," I said. "She's notoriously impatient. I'll go distract her while you finish."

I hurried through the swinging doors—then stopped short when I saw Logan standing there. His hands were shoved into the pockets of his jeans, and he was staring at the pies in the bakery case.

"Logan!" I blurted out in surprise.

"Hey," he said, stepping over to the counter. "I was hoping you'd be working here today. I was just wondering—um, remember how I was talking about getting a dog?"

"Yeah?" I was all too aware of Uncle Rick standing by the register. Close enough to hear every word. Luckily, my mom was out near the door chatting with the old ladies as they prepared to leave.

"So I was thinking of going to the animal shelter this weekend," Logan said. "Maybe Saturday? I was thinking maybe you could come with and help me pick something out." He grinned. "You know, since you're a dog expert, at least compared to me."

I just stared at him for a second. Susannah's advice was way too fresh in my head, confusing me. What was happening here? Was he asking me out? Or was this a just-friends thing? Or a just-friends thing that could turn into a date? Or—

"S-Saturday?" I said. "Um, I'm not sure. I have kickball practice that afternoon."

"Kickball?" He looked surprised.

I nodded. "There's this big rivalry between the high school and the college, and I'm on the high school team, and—"

I jumped as the bell jingled and Megan hurried in. She spotted Logan right away and made a beeline for us.

"Logan!" she exclaimed. "What are you doing here?" She shot me a slightly suspicious look. "Bailey? Is my special order ready yet?"

"I'll go check." Without another glance at Logan, I turned and rushed back to the kitchen. Susannah was just packing the cupcake into a tiny cardboard box. "Megan's here," I said.

"Here you go." Susannah handed me the box.

"Can you take it out to her?" I asked. "Logan just came in."

Susannah's eyes lit up. "Really? Cool, I want to check this guy out. I didn't pay much attention to him yesterday."

"Wait." I grabbed the box out of her hand. "Never mind, I'll do it." The last thing I needed was for Susannah to start talking me up to Logan in front of Megan.

She winked. "Suit yourself."

I took a deep breath before I headed back out there. As I pushed through the swinging doors, I pasted a pleasant smile on my face. It wavered a little when I saw that Megan had her hand on Logan's arm, and he was smiling at her. But I fought back the urge to turn around and run away.

"Here you go," I told Megan, setting the cupcake box on the counter. "That'll be, uh . . ." I stared at the cash register, suddenly unable to remember how much a single cupcake cost. Curse Methuselah and his old-fashioned ways, which required me to punch in actual numbers! Next chance I got, I was going to petition my family to put in a modern register, like the ones in the fast-food places where all you had to do was hit a key with a picture of a cupcake on it.

As I stared helplessly at the register's keys, Uncle Rick wandered closer. "Forget that, Bailey. It's on the house." He winked at Megan. "Friends-and-family discount."

"Thanks!" Megan beamed at Uncle Rick, then picked up the box and turned to Logan. "Ready to go?"

"Um, sure, I guess." Logan turned to me. "See you in bio tomorrow, Bailey?"

"Right. See you," I said, careful to keep that pleasant smile on my face until they were both out the door.

Chapter❀Ten

When I emerged from the house on Tuesday morning, Simone was already at the bus stop. She leaned against the stop sign at the end of our block, her head bent over her phone as her thumbs flew over its tiny keyboard. She glanced up when I approached.

"You need to get together with Logan already, because Ling and Megan are driving me cray-cray," she announced.

"Forget it. Not happening." I dropped my backpack at my feet and stifled a yawn. I hadn't slept well the night before—I'd kept waking up with vague memories of bizarre dreams. It was probably the full moon. I'd read an interesting abstract recently about a study in Europe showing some preliminary links between moon cycles and sleep patterns.

"No, seriously. Ling called me last night freaking out because Megan bought Logan a cupcake or something—"

"A custom welcome-to-town cupcake." It wasn't easy to keep the sarcasm out of my voice.

"Whatever. Anyway, Megan just texted me." She waved her phone for emphasis. "Now *she's* freaking out because Ling keeps hinting around about some big plans she supposedly has with Logan this weekend."

"Plans?" My mind immediately jumped to his animal-shelter invitation. "What plans?"

"How should I know?" Simone let out a loud snort. "If you ask me, Ling's probably just trying to make Megan jealous."

I wasn't so sure. Why had I acted like such a weirdo the day before when Logan had mentioned hitting up the animal shelter? It wasn't as if he'd asked me out on some romantic date. It could have been the perfect way to follow Susannah's advice. Not to mention fun. And now Ling was probably going to have that fun instead of me. Not fair.

"Did you finish the social-studies homework?" I asked, hoping to change the subject. "The last two questions were kind of tricky."

"Yeah, I did it." Simone waved a hand to brush away the new topic. "But listen—you really need to jump in and save Logan from those two before it's too late."

"Give it up, Simone. No means no."

She sighed. "I just don't get you, Bailey. For the first time in, like, ever, you actually like a guy. And you're too stubborn to admit it!"

"It's not about admitting it. It's about living in the real world, not some fantasy romance novel or something." I heard the clank and wheeze of the bus coming around the corner. "Now can we please stop talking about this? If I wanted to spill my guts about this particular topic, I'd post it on Facebook."

"Whatever." Simone frowned at me, then turned away to watch the bus approach. "I guess there's not much else to say about it anyway."

Zoe and Taylor were at our usual meeting spot when Simone and I arrived at school. Zoe was trying to keep her geometry book spinning on one finger, while Taylor was leaning against the wall picking at her cuticles.

"Where are the others?" Simone asked.

Zoe stopped the book and started spinning it the other direction. "Ling dragged Logan off as soon as he turned up. Claimed she was dying to show him the view from the second-floor landing."

"Yeah." Taylor giggled. "When Megan got here and heard that, she stomped off to find them. She's probably trying to push Ling out the window as we speak."

"Oh, man." Simone shook her head and shot me a dark look.

I pretended I didn't notice. The last thing I wanted to do was set her off on another rant about me and Logan, especially in front of Taylor and Zoe.

Luckily, Matt and Darius arrived just then. That distracted

Simone just long enough for me to mutter an excuse about needing something from my locker and rush off to hide until homeroom.

There was no art class on Tuesdays or Thursdays, so I didn't see Logan until biology. When I walked into class, he was chatting with a couple of guys, but when he saw me sit down, he hurried over and slid into his own seat.

"Hey," he said. "Sorry I had to take off so fast yesterday. Megan . . ." Seeming at a loss for words, he just shrugged.

"No problem, I don't have much time to chat at work anyway." I avoided meeting his gaze, instead focusing on unpacking my books.

"Aw, come on, really?" His tone was light and teasing. "I bet the owners might let you take a break sometimes if you ask them nicely."

Why did he have to do that? Why did he have to talk to me in that maybe-we're-friends, maybe-we're-flirting kind of way? I wasn't used to that sort of thing. It confused me, made me start to think (again) that maybe Simone was right about all this.

But I knew she wasn't. Seeing Logan with Megan yesterday had driven that home. I'd been right to think Logan and I were better off being friends.

And it was just as well, really. Much less pressure that way. No need to adjust my life plans. All I had to do was focus on being friends with Logan—*just* friends—and ignore all that silly spark stuff until it went away.

Starting now.

I forced a smile. "Megan's great, isn't she?" I said. "She and I are really good friends."

"Uh, sure, she's nice. She thinks you're great too."

"Yeah. She's not just a pretty face, either." I put as much enthusiasm as I could into my words. "She's got a beautiful singing voice, and a great sense of humor."

Logan didn't say anything. Out of the corner of my eye I could see him staring at me with a perplexed look on his face.

Just then Megan herself hurried in, followed a second later by Mr. Ba. The class quieted down immediately, all eyes focused on the stack of papers the teacher was holding.

"Oh, man!" Andy Menendez called out from the seat in front of Logan. "Don't tell me we're getting those tests back already? I was hoping to live a little longer before my parents kill me."

Mr. Ba smiled. "No such respite for you, Mr. Menendez. My phylogenetics seminar was postponed, so I found myself with some extra time for grading last night." He waved the papers. "Most of you did fine. Some of you did not. I won't keep you in suspense."

He started passing out the papers. After he dropped Andy's test on his desk, the teacher paused and glanced at Logan. "Mr. Morse," he said. "I nearly forgot about you. Can I trust you not to take a peek at your neighbors' papers? I don't want to have to make up an entirely new test for you next week."

"Scout's honor." Logan raised his right hand in a loose salute. "I'm not a cheater."

"I'm glad to hear it." Mr. Ba winked at him as he stepped past his desk to mine. Shuffling through the papers in his hand, he pulled one out and dropped it in front of me. "Nice work, Bailey."

"Thanks." I beamed at the bright red A at the top of my paper, everything else momentarily forgotten.

I was still riding high on that A as I walked to lunch with my friends, though I was trying not to celebrate too obviously. Not that they'd flunked or anything, thank goodness. Simone had scored a B, which seemed to make her happy enough, and Taylor had been relieved to squeak by with a C-minus. I wasn't sure what grade Megan had gotten yet, but since she'd stayed behind to discuss it with Mr. Ba instead of walking to lunch with us, I figured it couldn't have been too good.

"Glad it's finally lunchtime," Logan commented as we walked. "I'm starved."

Oh. Did I mention that Logan was one of the friends I was walking to lunch with? Somehow he'd just fallen into step with us, even waiting while Taylor stopped to grab her lunch out of her locker.

"Don't you need to hit your locker, Bailey?" Logan asked as we turned toward the cafeteria.

"I didn't have time to pack anything this morning," I replied. "Guess I'm stuck with cafeteria slop today."

"Really?" He smiled. "I pictured you bringing delicious gourmet sandwiches from your family's place every day."

"I know, right?" Simone linked her arm through mine. "I've been trying to convince her parents to start catering at school so we don't keep getting poisoned by the mystery meat."

Logan laughed. "Whoa, makes me wish I'd slapped together a PB and J myself this morning."

"The food's not that bad," I assured him. "The ambulance only has to come a couple of times a month."

That made everyone laugh. I grinned, still feeling a little giddy thanks to that A. "After you," Logan said as we reached the cafeteria, standing back to let me go through the door first.

"What a gentleman," Taylor said, sweeping past him as well. She shook her lunch bag. "See you guys at the table."

It was too noisy to do much talking in the lunch line. When the three of us emerged holding our trays, Simone glanced at Logan. "You're eating with us, right?" she said, her tone indicating it was a rhetorical question.

"Guys! Wait up!"

I turned and saw Ling hurrying toward us. She didn't have a tray, just an apple and a carton of chocolate milk—her favorite. The girl was obsessed with chocolate to the point she claimed she'd go into a coma if she didn't have some every day. (Not medically plausible, by the way.) Whenever she came to Eats, it was practically guaranteed that my dad would have to order more baking chocolate and cocoa powder from our supplier.

"Hi, Ling," I greeted her, my heart sinking as I saw the way she was looking at Logan. Like a fox stalking a squirrel. A poor, innocent, surprisingly good-looking squirrel.

"Can you believe the dog chow they're passing off as food today?" Ling glanced at Simone's tray and wrinkled her nose. Then she turned to Logan and smiled. "I hope they warned you that you're taking your life into your hands trying to eat the food here—especially the beef stew."

Logan chuckled. "Hey, I've eaten boiled caterpillars in Botswana and fried eel skin in Singapore." He patted his stomach. "Cafeteria food doesn't scare me."

Ling looked horrified for a second, then giggled. "Oh, Logan! You're such a goof."

I walked faster. My stomach was churning, and it had nothing to do with what Logan had said. Or with the cafeteria food.

Taylor and Megan were at our usual table, along with Zoe, Matt, and Darius. Darius was juggling several tater tots, which was making Megan giggle. But when she saw us coming, her expression went sharp.

"Hey, Ling," Megan said. "I thought you were going to get rid of those jeans. Because you were right—they're super unflattering."

Ling opened her milk carton and took a sip, not even glancing down at her jeans—which, by the way, fit her perfectly and looked great, like everything else she wore. "Nice shirt, Megs," she said. "Did you get it at the thrift store? It looks like one I donated two years ago."

Megan touched her shirt. "Actually, I got it at that fancy new boutique at the mall." Her voice was syrupy sweet, but her green eyes flashed dangerously. "Not that I'd expect you to recognize it, babe. I know that place is too pricey for you." She turned and flashed a smile at Logan, patting the chair beside her. "Hey, Logan, I saved you a seat."

Logan paused in the middle of setting his tray down next to Matt's. "Oh, uh, thanks." He slid the tray across the table, then squeezed behind Megan to get to the chair.

"Got space over there for me?" Ling followed him, holding her open carton aloft as she pushed past Megan's chair. "Oops!" she cried, lurching forward.

"Hey!" Megan jumped to her feet as chocolate milk spilled down the front of her shirt.

I gasped, shooting a quick glance at Simone, who looked stunned. Even Matt and Darius had gone silent.

"Oh, no!" Zoe exclaimed. "Megan, your shirt!"

Normally, Megan loved being stared at, but today she looked ready to cry. Or scream. Or possibly kill somebody—specifically Ling.

"Oops! Sorry." Ling didn't sound sorry at all as she slipped into the seat on Logan's other side. "You'd better go to the bathroom and blot that, or it'll stain."

Megan gnashed her teeth, and for a second I was afraid she was going to go all WrestleMania on Ling right then and there.

Instead she took a deep breath and shot Logan a rather pained smile. "Be right back." Without a word to the rest of us, she climbed to her feet and stalked off toward the restrooms.

"I'd better go see if she needs help." Taylor shot Ling a nervous look, then scurried after Megan.

I just sighed and dug into my not-confirmed-to-be-actual-beef stew. Now that I'd accepted that Logan and I weren't meant to be together, I only hoped my friends would hurry up and figure out which of them was going to get him so we could all move on with our lives with a minimum of drama and destruction.

By Wednesday I was almost getting used to thinking of Logan as a friend and nothing more. I had a yearbook meeting before school, so I didn't see him then. When I emerged from first period, I didn't even stop outside the classroom and scan the halls for him so we could walk to art class together. Okay, I *thought* about doing that. But I didn't. That was progress, right?

Logan hadn't arrived yet when I walked into art. Gabi and Gwen were in their usual spots. They glanced up when I reached the table.

"Hey, where's lover boy?" Gabi asked. "Didn't he walk you to class today? And carry your books, and offer to buy you a soda pop after school?"

"Very funny." I dropped my backpack and sat down.

"Seriously, are you and Logan a couple now or what?" Gwen put in. "Because if you are, maybe you could whisper sweet nothings in his ear about trying out for the play."

Out of the corner of my eye I saw Logan entering. "Shh!" I hissed at the two girls. "No, we're not a couple. We're just friends."

The two of them traded a skeptical look. "Whatever you say," Gabi said.

"Yeah." Gwen smirked. "Lover girl."

"Hi." Logan reached the table and grinned at all three of us. "This seat taken?"

"It's all yours, lov—" A sharp kick from Gabi under the table cut Gwen off midword. When Logan gave her a perplexed look, she smiled sheepishly. "Uh, luv," she said. "It's a British thing."

"Yeah," Gabi put in helpfully. "She's calling everyone that today. Right, luv?"

"Totally, luv." Gwen grinned at Logan. "So listen, luv. Did I mention we're casting *Camelot* next week?"

When I entered bio that day, Logan was at the front of the room talking to Mr. Ba. I couldn't hear what they were saying, though Logan's expression was serious. He nodded a few times, then hurried over to take his seat.

"Is everything okay?" I asked. "You look kind of freaked out."

For a second I felt proud of myself. That was exactly what I would have said to any of my friends in the same situation. Any of my *other* friends. Since that was what Logan was. A friend. See how well I was doing?

"Mr. Ba changed the plan," he said with a frown.

"Yeah, he does that. 'Nothing is constant but change.'"

"Huh?" He blinked at me.

"It's one of his favorite quotes." I glanced at Mr. Ba, who was wiping the last period's lesson off the whiteboard. "Never mind. What plan do you mean?"

"Remember how he was going to have me take that test next week? Now he wants me to take some kind of placement test instead." Logan swallowed hard. "Tomorrow."

"A placement test?"

Logan nodded. "He says he wants to figure out what I know. And whether I should stay in this class or maybe transfer to a different one."

"Transfer?" My mind reeled at the very thought. This was the only class the two of us had together every day!

Whoops. That wasn't how a friend would react, was it? He'd already admitted he wasn't that great at science. This was the toughest class open to sophomores, and we were already halfway through the semester. Maybe it *would* be better for him to switch to an easier class. Was that what a friend would suggest?

He didn't give me much time to think about it. "I need to stay in this class," he said, his voice low and urgent. "Will you—could you help me study for the placement test? We have that study hall today. . . ."

His eyes were very blue as he gazed at me hopefully. I only hesitated for a second.

"Sure," I said. "Of course."

"Awesome!" He grinned and raised his hand for a high five. "I really appreciate it, Bailey."

"No problem." I slapped his hand lightly, trying not to second-guess myself. After all, I'd be happy to help any other student who asked for it. Why not my new friend Logan?

Chapter ✺ Eleven

know it was her!" Ling fumed. "I mean, what is she, five years old?"

It was Wednesday afternoon, and Ling and I were in our fifth-period geometry class. Usually I liked sitting with Ling in our regular seats at the back of the room. She was always making sarcastic little quips that made me laugh and kept me awake during Mr. Feeney's boring lectures about the Pythagorean theorem.

Today? Not so much. All she could talk about was her escalating war with Megan. Specifically, a rumor making the rounds today that Ling had just been diagnosed with mononucleosis.

"You know what they call mono, right?" Ling said quietly, checking to make sure Feeney was still writing on the board.

"The kissing disease! Megan's obviously trying to make Logan think I'm out there kissing random people left and right."

"That's not the only way you can get mono," I pointed out. "You can get it if you drink from the same glass as an infected person, or share a fork, or stuff like that."

She turned to me, eyebrows arched. "Not the point, Bailey."

"Okay, okay." I really wished she'd stop talking about this. The last words I wanted to hear in the same sentence were Logan and kissing. Well, Logan and kissing and Ling. Or Megan. Or anyone else except maybe . . .

No. I had to keep my imagination under control. Logan and I were friends. And friends did *not* kiss. Or even think about kissing. One friend certainly didn't wonder if the other friend's lips were as soft as they looked. . . .

Okay, now I could feel my face turning red. I sank down in my seat, trying to hide my consternation from Ling.

No such luck. The girl notices everything. Especially the stuff you don't want her to notice.

"What's the matter with you?" she demanded. "Your face is going all blotchy."

"Really?" I forced a cough. "Uh-oh, maybe I'm coming down with something. Wouldn't it be ironic if it was mono?"

"Well, don't breathe on me just in case." She scooted her chair a little farther away.

"You can't actually get mono from . . . never mind," I said.

Ling glanced at Mr. Feeney again, then leaned back toward

me. "Anyway, you have study hall with Logan today, right? If you get a chance to bring it up, tell him those rumors definitely aren't true, okay? And tell him Megan's a psycho while you're at it."

Just then Mr. Feeney turned around and started blabbing about Euclid, saving me from having to answer.

When I emerged from sixth-period English, I found Simone lurking outside the door. "What are you doing here?" I asked. "Didn't you just have Spanish on the other side of the building?"

"I told Señora Garcia I had cramps so she'd let me leave early." She grabbed my arm and dragged me in the direction of the girls' bathroom. "I wanted to be here in case you need my help touching up before study hall."

"What? Why would I need to touch up before study hall?"

"I'm just saying, a little blush and some eyeliner wouldn't kill you." Simone patted her bag, which I knew contained a plethora of makeup options. "You're so pretty, Bailey. If you'd play up your best features just a teensy bit more, you'd be even more gorgeous."

"I hate to disappoint you, but Logan and I are going to be studying bio, not gazing into each other's eyes—lined or not." I shook my arm loose before we reached the bathroom door. "And we're going to need all the time we can get, so I don't want to waste any of it primping."

"Oh, I see." She smiled and stepped back. "Can't wait even one extra minute to see him, huh?"

"Whatever." I rolled my eyes. "Are you coming or not?"

I tried not to let her see how nervous I felt as we walked down the hall. Mostly because I knew I shouldn't *be* nervous. It wasn't as if this was the first time I'd helped a friend through a bio crisis. Far from it. Simone and the other girls asked me to help them study all the time. This was just like that. Right?

Logan was at his desk talking to Taylor when we came in. He jumped out of his seat when he saw me, his smile looking a little wobbly around the edges.

"Hey, Bailey," he said as I dropped my bag onto my usual desk. "You, um, didn't forget about helping me study, did you?"

"She definitely didn't." Simone plucked at Taylor's sleeve. "These two are actually going to be hitting the books, so we might as well go find someone else to talk to."

"Really?" Taylor looked surprised.

"I know, right? Studying in study hall—who ever heard of that?" Simone gave me and Logan a little wave. "Later, guys."

The two of them hurried off. I sat down and pulled out my bio textbook. "Should we get started?"

"Yeah, okay." Logan flipped open his own textbook, then cleared his throat. "Listen, I really appreciate this, Bailey. I don't know what I'll do if I don't pass this test."

"It's no big deal," I said. "You can always transfer into an easier section. Or even into earth science. Zoe says it's actually pretty interesting."

"No, I can't." His words came out surprisingly sharp.

I guess he noticed my surprise, because he immediately looked sheepish. "Sorry for snapping like that. It's just . . ." He sighed and rubbed his forehead. "I don't know, maybe it's stupid."

"What?" I wasn't sure why he looked so stressed all of a sudden.

"It's my parents. They've never come right out and said they expect me to get straight As or anything, but . . ."

"You don't want to disappoint them?" I nodded. "Been there. Still doing that."

"Really?" He glanced at me, looking surprised.

I smiled. "Just because they run a restaurant, it doesn't mean they aren't going to be disappointed in us if we can barely write out the specials board or add up a check."

"Oh!" He looked pained. "I'm sorry, Bailey. I didn't mean—"

"It's cool, I'm just teasing you," I said quickly. "But seriously, my mom was a straight A student herself, and Dad thinks education is super important. They definitely expect my sister and me to keep our grades up."

"Right, same. And the thing is, it's pretty easy for me to do well in most of my classes. It's just that the past couple of years, the science and math classes have been getting harder and harder, and well . . ." He let out a hollow chuckle. "It's starting to make me wonder if I even fit in in my own family." He slid his eyes toward me. "That probably sounds really lame."

"No, it doesn't. Trust me, I get it. My family's the same way. Everyone just assumes all the kids will grow up and work at Eats, but I've known since I was little that I didn't want to do that. I can't even imagine spending my whole life making sandwiches and scheduling produce deliveries and stuff."

"Do they know that?" Logan asked. "Your parents, I mean."

"Yeah." I shrugged. "But I can tell they don't really get it."

"Bummer."

"No, it's okay. They still support me and everything. It just feels a little weird sometimes when I realize I really am different from them." I bit my lip, glancing across the room at Simone and Taylor. Now that I thought about it, I could've said the exact same thing about my friends.

Logan looked thoughtful. "I know what you mean," he said. "Whenever I mess up at something sciencey, I start to wonder if they switched babies at the hospital when I was born or something." He smiled. "Except that I definitely have my dad's ears, so I guess not."

I smiled back. For a second we just sat there smiling at each other. He really was a great guy, even if he wasn't a science genius like his parents.

Which reminded me. Sitting here staring at each other and talking about our families wasn't going to help him pass that test.

"Okay," I said, trying to sound businesslike as I pulled my bio textbook closer and flipped through the pages. "Let's get down to work."

"Thanks again for the ride, Dad," I said as my father steered into the school's drop-off zone on Thursday morning. The buses hadn't arrived yet, so only a few people were hanging out by the flagpole.

"You're welcome." Dad yawned as he threw the car into neutral. "Gives me an excuse to be late so someone else has to clean out the coffee pots."

I smiled. "See you after school."

"Don't be late. Faculty meeting at the law school today, which always means a rush on coffee and pastries." He reached over and tousled my hair. "Have a good day, Bailey."

I took a few deep breaths of the cool morning air as I hurried up the school steps, trying to keep my mind on the task at hand. Logan and I had made a lot of progress the day before in study hall. I was still a little surprised by how much trouble he had with some pretty basic concepts, like the difference between a gene and an allele or how cell division worked. Hadn't he learned anything from living with his parents all those years? But he was trying, and by the time the bell rang I felt pretty confident that he'd be able to squeak by.

When he'd begged me to meet him before homeroom for a little more cramming, though, how could I say no? That was why I'd asked Dad to drop me off on his way to work. My bus often didn't get in until ten minutes before the bell.

Of course, when I'd told Simone, she'd seemed to think it was some kind of date. I was lucky she hated waking up any earlier than she absolutely had to. Otherwise she probably would have shown up that morning wanting to cram me into a ball gown and heels.

And that definitely wasn't what this was about. I was totally focused on getting Logan through this test. I'd spent over an hour after dinner last night planning out what we needed to review to ensure that he could go into it feeling confident.

I stopped at my locker just long enough to shed my jacket and grab a few books. Then I headed for the library, which was where Logan and I had agreed to meet.

After Mr. Ba's classroom, the library was my favorite spot in the entire school. It had been renovated and expanded a few years earlier. There was a big central atrium with lots of natural light and huge wooden tables where people could study, a whole row of computer monitors along the outside walls, and tidy rows of books beyond that.

As I pushed through the big glass doors, I could already see Logan sitting at one of the pine-topped tables. But he wasn't alone.

He spotted me right away and raised one hand in a wave. "Bailey!" he called out. "Over here."

Ling looked up and smiled as I approached. "Oh, hi, Bailey," she said. "I was just about to text you to say you could sleep in after all."

"What?" I was still so focused on my study plans that it took me a moment to clue in to what was going on.

Ling reached over and put a hand on Logan's arm. "Logan was just telling me about that placement test. Since I was here, I figured I'd help him study."

"You—huh?" I blinked at her. The "since I was here" part wasn't so strange. Ling lived five blocks from school and was a morning person. She was often at school before the rest of us.

No, the weird part was "I figured I'd help him study." Not that Ling was stupid—far from it. She was one of those people who got good-to-excellent grades without having to expend much effort. Translation? She hardly ever actually studied for anything. And often mocked those of us who did. In other words, not what most people would consider an ideal tutor for a struggling student.

"I said I'm *helping him study*." She enunciated each word carefully.

I still wasn't quite taking this in. "But you're not even in our class."

"So what? I have Mr. Ba for first period, remember?" There was a hint of annoyance in her smile now. I knew she was losing patience with me—expecting me to back off and let her do her thing.

Usually when Ling got that look on her face, it was best to let her have her way. Otherwise things tended to get messy.

Still, I hesitated. After talking with Logan the day before, I knew how important this was to him. He didn't need Ling flirting instead of helping right now. Even if she did actually try to help him study, there was only so much she could do—while she *was* in one of Mr. Ba's other tenth-grade bio classes, it wasn't an accelerated class like ours.

Logan spoke up. "It's cool, Ling. I need all the help I can get. Maybe all three of us can study together?"

"What a good idea." She shot him a brilliant smile. "Oops, except I just remembered something—I passed Zoe on my way here, and she was looking for Bailey. Said she left something important in your locker yesterday." She shot me a meaningful look.

For a second I felt stubborn. Why should I let Ling chase me away? *She* was the one who was butting in on *my* plans, not the other way around.

Then again, what did it matter? I'd already done my job. Logan knew the material—anything we could cover this morning would only be a review. Maybe it was a good thing if Ling could distract him from stressing out about the test for a while.

And if that was the case, I shouldn't mind stepping aside. Not unless this meeting was more to me than a study session. Which it wasn't. Logan and I were just friends. I needed to remember that.

"Oh. Okay, yeah." I took a step backward, clutching my biology textbook to my chest. "I'd better go see what Zoe wants."

"Are you sure?" Logan looked anxious.

Avoiding his eye, I backed up another step. "Yeah. Ling can help you—it'll be fine."

I turned and scurried away without a backward look.

"Ugh. I hate when Mr. Ba makes us touch mold." Simone squirted another dollop of soap onto her palm. "It never feels like I can get it all off my hands."

We were scrubbing up after that day's bio lab. It had been an interesting one involving some mold spores we'd been growing since the beginning of the month. But for once I hadn't been able to focus. I was all too aware that Logan was up there beyond the sliding doors in the classroom side of the room taking his placement test.

"Yeah," I said, still distracted. "Eau de Rhizopus Stolonifer. It's the next hot thing."

Simone laughed, then reached for a paper towel. "Let's get out of here."

We grabbed our stuff and exited into the hall through the door at the back of the lab area. My gaze shot immediately to the other door—the one leading into the classroom area. It was closed. That meant Logan was still taking his test.

Simone hoisted her backpack onto one shoulder. "Ready to head to lunch?" she asked.

"You go ahead." I shot another glance at the closed classroom door. "I want to wait and see how Logan did."

"Oh, right." Simone immediately gave me a critical once-over, then fluffed up my hair and straightened my shirt. "Want me to wait with you?"

"No, go ahead. No sense both of us being late for lunch." I tried to sound casual.

"You want to be alone with him, huh? Okay." She smirked. "I'll try to keep Ling from rushing over here to offer her assistance."

I'd told her about that morning's library situation, of course.

She'd been horrified but unsurprised. The war between Ling and Megan was still escalating—the two of them were barely speaking except to trade the occasional insult.

As Simone hurried off toward the cafeteria, I stepped over and peeked in through the glass part of the classroom door. Logan was bent over his test paper, face scrunched up with concentration. Mr. Ba was at his desk and saw me looking in. I stepped back quickly, but a moment later the teacher opened the door and joined me in the hall.

"Did you need something, Bailey?" he asked.

"No, sorry," I said. "I was just seeing if Logan was finished yet."

"Not yet." Mr. Ba glanced at the door. "He got permission to stay a few extra minutes if necessary, since he has lunch period next. I'm happy to see that he's taking this placement test very seriously."

"Oh, he definitely is!" The words came out sounding a little more passionate than I'd intended. Clearing my throat, I added, "Um, I mean, Logan really wants to stay in this class."

"Yes." Mr. Ba stroked his chin, studying me with his perceptive dark eyes. "I can see that he's a very driven and intelligent young man. I'm not surprised, given his lineage."

"You mean his parents?" I said. "Do you know his mother?"

"Of course. Everyone at the university is thrilled to have Dr. Morse join the faculty. She's done some groundbreaking research in quantum thermodynamics," Mr. Ba replied. "I know Logan's father only by reputation. But I understand he's one of the top scholars in his field."

"Yeah, that was my impression too."

Mr. Ba nodded. "I imagine it would be difficult for a non-science-oriented child to grow up in that sort of household." He chuckled. "Rather like a tone-deaf child being raised by Mozart and Leontyne Price, eh?"

"I don't think Logan's *that* bad at science," I protested. "I was helping him prep for the test in study hall yesterday, and he caught on to most of the stuff pretty fast."

"That's good to hear." Mr. Ba smiled. "Don't worry, Bailey. I promise you that I'm invested in the academic improvement of *all* my students. Not just the talented ones like you."

"I know. But—"

"*But,*" he interrupted, holding up one long, slim finger, "if the results of the placement test show that what's best for Logan is to transfer to a less advanced class, that's what I'll recommend." He checked his watch. "Now, you'd better scurry along to lunch."

Despite Mr. Ba's comment, I actually felt sort of optimistic as I headed for the cafeteria. Logan knew the material, and he was definitely motivated. He'd pass that test and then everything would be fine.

That sense of optimism lasted until Logan walked over to our lunch table and collapsed into the empty seat between Megan and Ling, looking totally wiped out. "Logan!" Ling exclaimed. "How'd it go?"

"Okay, I guess." Logan smiled, but it looked forced.

"Was there anything about homeostasis on the test?" I asked.

That was the one area that had given him the most trouble in yesterday's study session.

"Two questions." He lifted one shoulder. "I'm pretty sure I got the second one right, but the first one was kind of tricky."

"Never mind, I'm sure you did great," Megan broke in, scooting her chair closer to his. "Now listen, Logan, we were just talking about that new action movie that opens this weekend."

"We were?" Darius glanced at Matt and shrugged. "I must've missed that."

Meanwhile Ling was glaring at Megan. "Do you mind?" she snapped. "Logan was right in the middle of telling us about his test!" She put a hand on his. "Go ahead, Logan."

"No, it's okay." He dumped his bagged lunch out on the table and picked up a banana. "I don't really want to talk about it anymore."

"See?" Megan rolled her eyes at Ling. "So anyway, about that movie . . ."

Chapter ● Twelve

By Friday morning I still wasn't sure how Logan had really done on that placement test. "I just hope he passed," I told Simone as the two of us climbed off the bus. "If he didn't, he's really going to beat himself up about it."

She shot me a sympathetic look. We'd been discussing the Logan situation all the way to school.

"It'll be a bummer if he has to transfer out of our class," she said. "You'll hardly get to see him."

"That's not the point," I protested.

She yanked open the school door. "Seems like at least part of the point to me. How are you going to get to know him better if you never spend any time together?" She grimaced. "Especially with Megan and Ling hogging his attention at lunch. I swear, those two are driving me crazy! Why can't they see how obvious it is that you're the one Logan is meant to be with?"

"Because there's nothing to see." I glanced around, making sure nobody was close enough to hear us. "I'm not *meant to be* with Logan."

"But the sparks!" she began.

"Sparks don't mean anything. That stuff I felt was just a typical hormonal teenage reaction to a good-looking guy. Just a remnant of our primordial past when humans had to mate quickly before we got eaten by dinosaurs."

She gave me a strange look. Clearly she didn't get scientific humor.

"Right," she said. "You just happened to have that reaction to this particular guy—for the first time ever."

"You don't know that," I retorted. "Maybe I react that way to every guy I see, and I just never told you about it before."

She didn't look convinced. "I just don't see why you won't at least consider this. What are you afraid of?"

"How about Ling and Megan?" That was supposed to be a joke too, though it actually didn't seem very funny. "Besides, Logan and I don't have enough in common. I mean, how can I go out with a guy who barely knows a cell from a cell phone?"

By then we were almost to our morning meeting spot. Megan, Ling, and Zoe were there already.

"Happy Friday," Zoe greeted us. "Can we go home yet?"

"I wish." Ling held out a hand to check her manicure. "Have

you guys seen Logan yet? I need to find out if he's going to be around this weekend."

"Wait, I thought you were so sure you'd be hanging out with him all weekend?" Megan smirked. "What happened—did he turn you down?"

"Of course not," Ling snapped. "He's saving up all his rejections for you."

Megan rolled her eyes. "Oh, please."

"Do *you* have weekend plans with Logan?" Simone asked her.

Megan frowned. "Not yet. But Logan and I were talking in homeroom yesterday about how nice the weather's supposed to be tomorrow, and I'm sure he's planning to ask me out."

Simone shot me a look. "So *neither* of you has nailed down any plans with Logan this weekend. Interesting."

"Why do you say that?" Now Ling was frowning at Simone too. "Don't tell me *you're* still interested in him?"

"*I* was never interested in Logan." Simone shrugged. "The more relevant issue, though, is that Logan doesn't seem particularly interested in either of you. Don't you agree, Bailey?"

I shot her a warning look. "Leave me out of this, Simone."

"Yeah. Mind your own business, Simone," Ling added.

"Shut up, all of you—here he comes!" Megan hissed. Then she stepped forward and waved. "Hi, Logan!"

Logan was walking toward us with Matt and Darius. "Aren't you going to say hi to me?" Darius asked Megan with a grin.

She rolled her eyes. "Okay, hi, whatever." Then she turned

back to Logan. "So what's up? Do anything interesting last night?"

Logan looked slightly confused. "Homework, dinner—the usual," he said. "Why? Did I miss a big party or something?"

"Don't listen to her." Ling grabbed him by the arm. "She's always a little random in the morning." She tossed her hair and giggled loudly, even though she hadn't said anything remotely funny.

"Whatever." Megan shot Ling a poisonous look, then sidled closer to Logan. "So Logan, I really like that shirt. Where'd you get it?"

"I'm not sure." He glanced down at his shirt, a perfectly ordinary brown henley. "I think my mom bought it for me?"

"Hey, Darius, I just loooove your shoes," Matt said, making a goofy face. "Wherever did you get them?"

"Dude, thanks!" Darius grinned. "And I just adore your sweat socks. They're *fabulous*!"

Megan glared at the guys as Zoe and Simone laughed. Personally, I couldn't blame them for making fun of her. She and Ling had never gone so psycho over a guy before. Obviously, competition was bringing out the worst in both of them.

Logan was staring at the other two guys, obviously not getting the joke. Feeling bad for him, I cleared my throat. "Hey, Logan. Did you talk to Mr. Ba? Did he give you the results?"

"Haven't seen him yet." His expression turned anxious, making me wish I hadn't brought it up. "To be honest, I'm kind of afraid to go ask him. I figure I'll just wait and get the bad news in bio."

"That's the spirit, man!" Matt clapped him on the shoulder.

"Don't worry about it, Logan," Ling cooed. "Let's talk about something else. Like how fabulous the weather is supposed to be tomorrow, for instance . . ."

Logan was standing outside Mr. Ba's classroom when I arrived for bio class. "Hey," he greeted me, looking pale and sort of sick. "I was waiting for you. You know—for moral support. Wish me luck?"

"Of course! But you don't need it—I'm sure you did fine." I reached out and squeezed his hand.

Then I froze, realizing what I'd done. I snatched my hand back, my face flaming. What was I thinking? Yes, Logan and I were supposed to be friends. I'd acted on instinct, trying to make him feel better the same way I might have if this were Simone or one of the other girls standing in front of me.

But Logan wasn't Simone. He was still a guy. I couldn't just go around *touching* him!

He was looking at me, not saying anything. Our eyes met; his looked less nervous than they had a moment ago. Now they were curious. Or was that confused?

"Bailey, I . . . ," he began. Then he paused, glancing around at the students hurrying past in all directions.

I realized I was holding my breath, waiting for him to continue. To react to what I'd done. My heart beat faster. . . .

Then the door swung open and Mr. Ba peered out. "Logan! There you are," the teacher said. "Can you give us a moment, please, Bailey?"

"Sure." I pretended to fiddle with my backpack as Mr. Ba led Logan a few yards down the hall.

The conversation didn't take very long. I couldn't hear what Mr. Ba was saying, but I saw Logan's face fall as the teacher talked. Uh-oh—that couldn't be good news. He nodded a few times as Mr. Ba continued to talk, though he still looked upset.

Then, to my surprise, Mr. Ba called me over to join them. "Bailey," he said briskly, "Mr. Morse and I would like to talk to you about something."

"Okay." I shifted my backpack farther up my shoulder. "What is it?"

Mr. Ba glanced at Logan. "Mr. Morse had some trouble with that placement test," he said. "Enough trouble that normally I'd recommend transferring to a different section. However, I can see that he's smart and motivated enough to do well in this class with a little extra help. That's where you come in."

I blinked and shot a look at Logan. What was Mr. Ba talking about?

He didn't leave me in suspense for long. "I know you helped Mr. Morse prepare for the test," he said. "I think continuing to study with someone like you would only benefit him. Would you be willing to tutor him on a regular basis to help him keep up with the class?"

"Tutor Logan? Sure!" I blurted out. "Um, I mean of course, that would be fine."

"Good, good." Mr. Ba smiled at both of us. "I understand the two of you have a study hall together. If you're willing to spend at least two of those periods per week working with Mr. Morse, I'm confident that he'll be able to handle this course."

"No problem! I can do all three days a week if you want." As soon as the words were out of my mouth, I realized they might sound a little too eager. "I mean, two days a week is fine. Or three. Whatever works."

"Thanks, Bailey." Logan sounded relieved. "Are you sure you don't mind? I know I'm a pretty tough case."

"I don't mind at all." Feeling my cheeks starting to go red as I met his eyes, I returned my gaze to Mr. Ba. "Really. It'll be fun."

"Good, good," Mr. Ba said again. "And of course, I'll make sure you get credit for peer tutoring on this semester's transcript, Bailey." He winked. "That should look good when you're applying for college down the road. And on the scholarship applications too."

I nodded. But for once I wasn't really thinking ahead to schools and scholarships. Instead a whole parade of images flitted through my head. Megan. Ling. The way Logan's hand had felt so warm and strong when I'd grabbed it just now . . .

Uh-oh. What had I just gotten myself into?

Chapter ● Thirteen

I was still nervous as I walked to study hall that afternoon. Simone wasn't helping.

"This is so cool, Bails!" she whispered as we headed for Mr. Gillespie's room. "You're going to have Logan's attention non-stop, three times a week. Megan and Ling will be so jealous when they find out!"

"Don't remind me." I glanced over my shoulder to make sure Logan wasn't walking up behind us in the hallway or something. "And yeah, I'll have his attention—talking about biology."

"Biology." Simone waggled her eyebrows. "The study of life. And living bodies. Especially *hot* living bodies."

I gave her a shove. "Quiet, we're here."

Logan was already in his seat when we entered. Simone waved

at him, then nudged me with her shoulder. "I'll leave you to it," she whispered. "Have fun!"

"Thanks." Tossing one last exasperated look at her, I headed for my seat beside Logan. I was nervous, but I tried not to let it show.

Logan had his bio book open in front of him. As I sat down, he sighed. "I'm glad you're here," he said. "I just started reading like thirty seconds ago, and I'm already confused." He swiped a hand through his hair, leaving a tuft standing up adorably in the front. "I'm starting to think it's a big mistake to try to stay in that class."

"No, it's not," I said quickly, my nerves dissipating in the face of a student in crisis. "You can do this, Logan. You know a lot more than you think you do. You just need a good review of what you already know, and a little confidence that you can learn the rest."

He bit his lip, glancing down at the book. "But what if I can't? My parents will freak if I come home with anything lower than a B."

"Then we'll have to make sure you get a B, right?" I shrugged. "Or better yet an A."

"Ah, so you're an optimist." The ghost of a smile flitted across his face.

"Yeah." I smiled back. "Plus, I love a challenge."

That actually made him laugh. "Okay, then let's see what you can do, Professor." He slid his desk over toward mine. It made a loud *skreek*ing noise against the linoleum floor, which caused everyone in the room to jump and turn to look at us.

I winced as I saw several people whisper and smile at each

other. What were they saying? Did they suspect my mind wasn't totally focused on biology? Well, at least not the kind in the textbook. I was careful not to look at Simone, who was giggling with Taylor near the front of the room.

Logan didn't seem to notice any of that. He lined up our desks beside each other, then pushed the textbook over so we could both see it.

"Where should we start?" he asked. "I studied the basics of cell theory last year, and I think I've got that down. But once you start getting into the chromosome stuff, I'm lost."

"Um, okay." I was a little distracted by how close he was. He smelled nice—like soap and almonds and laundry detergent. What about me? I tried to remember if I'd reapplied deodorant after gym. I was pretty sure I had, especially since I'd never forgotten before. Still, I carefully lifted one shoulder—the one farther away from Logan—and gave a subtle sniff.

Then I realized what I was doing. Namely, acting like an idiot. Had Logan noticed?

When I glanced over, his eyes were on the textbook as he paged through it. If I smelled funny, he wasn't letting it distract him.

"Where is it?" he muttered. "I know I just saw that part."

"Are you looking for the chapter on chromosomes? It's closer to the front—here." I reached for the book.

At the same time, he started to pull back. Our hands brushed against each other.

"Oops," he said.

"Sorry," I blurted out at the same time.

He pulled both his hands into his lap and leaned back in his chair. I leaned forward, trying to hide the blush I could feel creeping over my face as I flipped pages. It only took a few seconds to find the chapter I wanted, but I stayed in the same position, pretending to read over the first page while taking several deep (but quiet) breaths.

I needed to pull it together. This wasn't a date; it was a study session. If Logan was going to pass bio, let alone ace it, he needed help. Which meant I had to focus on the subject matter, not how nice he smelled or how tingly my hand felt where his had brushed it. Getting distracted by that stuff wasn't going to help anyone.

That brought me back to business. "Okay, chromosomes—chapter three," I said, making my voice as brisk and businesslike as possible. "So basically chromosomes are bundles of DNA . . ."

I didn't think about much other than biology until we came up for breath at the end of chapter five. "Okay, I think I've got it." Logan tapped his pen on the desk, scanning the study questions on the last page of the chapter. "Mitosis comes first, then cytokinesis." He shook his head and smiled. "It would help if all these terms didn't sound so much alike!"

"Never mind, you're getting it. So next we can move on to meiosis." I glanced at the clock and was surprised to see that the period was almost over. "Or maybe we can work on that next week."

He followed my gaze to the clock. "Probably a good thing. It'll take me all weekend to digest everything we just went over."

Despite his words, he sounded a lot more hopeful than he had at the beginning of study hall. We'd actually made a lot of progress in just one session. Maybe his mind wasn't built for science, exactly, but he was trying.

I shut the textbook. "Like I said, you're definitely getting it," I assured him. "Anyway, Mr. Ba wouldn't let you try if he thought it was a lost cause. He's pretty good at sizing people up."

"Yeah, I can tell." Logan slid the book into his backpack. "For one thing, he seems to think you're a scientific genius."

"I don't know about that." I grabbed my backpack so I could put away my pencils and stuff. "But Mr. Ba? Definitely a scientific genius. That's why I requested him as my academic advisor. I figured he could help me decide where to go to college."

Logan looked surprised. "I thought you were set on MIT."

"That's my first choice right now," I said. "But I can't count on getting in there. And even if I get in, I might not be able to go if I don't get some scholarships to help pay my way."

"Oh, right. You were talking about that before." Logan nodded. "I bet you'll get plenty of scholarships, though. Especially with Mr. Ba on your side." He grinned. "Not to mention your brilliant new career in tutoring high school science losers."

I smiled. "Which reminds me—I want you to read through

chapter six this weekend. That'll give us a head start on Monday."

"You got it, Professor." He sat back in his chair and stretched. "So speaking of the weekend, any big plans? What's up with that kickball thing you mentioned the other day?"

I was surprised he remembered that. "Yeah, I've got kickball practice tomorrow afternoon. Haven't the guys told you about the Co-Ed/Lo-Ed championship yet?"

"Nope."

"It's this crazy competition between the high school and the university," I explained. "I'm not even sure how long it's been going on—practically forever, I guess. My parents were both on the Lo-Ed team when they were in high school, and my dad played for the Co-Ed team too. . . ."

I went on to explain the whole tradition. Logan listened, looking amused.

"So the championship happens during this Spring Fling or whatever it's called?" he asked.

"Spring Thing. That's next weekend, which means *this* weekend is our last practice before the big game." I grinned. "Not that it makes that much difference whether we practice or not. The team takes anyone who wants to play, so needless to say we're not that hot."

He laughed. "Sounds like fun, though. What time's your practice tomorrow?"

"Two o'clock."

"So do you need to start psyching yourself up and stretching at the crack of dawn? Or would you maybe have time to hit the animal shelter with me in the morning?" He smiled. "I'm in desperate need of dog-choosing help, remember?"

"Oh yeah, you were going to go get a dog tomorrow, right?" Of course I remembered every word of our earlier conversation about the topic, but I tried not to let that show.

"Well, pick one out, anyway," he said, flicking a scrap of paper off the edge of his desk. "My parents can't make it tomorrow, but Dad said he'll take me in on Monday after school to sign the paperwork and stuff. We'll actually pick up the dog then. I called the shelter and they said that was cool—they'll hold a dog for up to three days."

"Don't your parents want to help pick it out?" I ask.

"Mom doesn't really have time, what with the new job and all." Logan shrugged. "And Dad says he's too much of a softy. If he had to choose, he says he'd come home with all of them."

I laughed. "Sounds like a good plan to me."

"Me too," Logan agreed. "But Mom is less of a fan. She's set a strict one dog limit. So that's why I need a second opinion."

I hesitated, still not quite sure what was going on here. Logan and I were just friends. But that was okay—this wasn't supposed to be a date or anything, right? Who ever heard of a date to an animal shelter?

He was waiting for an answer. "Okay," I said before I could overthink it anymore. "That sounds fun."

"Awesome." He looked pleased. "Ten thirty okay?"

"Sure. I'll meet you there."

The bell rang, sending the room into the usual end-of-day chaos. Logan grabbed his backpack and stood up. "Wow, I guess this means I officially survived my first week of school."

I laughed. "Congratulations."

We walked to the door. Simone and Taylor were there waiting. Logan said hi to them, then turned back toward me.

"Okay." He clutched the strap of his backpack, yanking on it restlessly. "I guess I'll see you tomorrow."

"Yeah. See you then."

He said good-bye to Simone and Taylor, then loped off down the hall. Simone spun to face me.

"Tomorrow?" she demanded eagerly. "He'll see you tomorrow? Spill!"

I sighed. "It's no big deal. He just needs my help picking out a dog at the shelter."

"Cute!" Taylor looked impressed. "That'll make an excellent first-date story to tell at your wedding someday."

I rolled my eyes. "It's not a first date. We're just friends."

"Yeah. Or that's what we'll be telling Ling and Megan, anyway, right?" Simone traded an amused look with Taylor.

Uh-oh. I'd almost forgotten about those two. "Don't tell them anything!" I begged. "Please? I really don't want to get in the middle of that. And like I said, this definitely isn't a date."

"Whatever." Simone linked her arm through mine, steering

me down the crowded hallway. "Your secret date is safe with us, isn't that so, Taylor?"

Taylor giggled. "Right! So what are you going to wear, Bailey?"

I sighed, once again wondering what I'd gotten myself into. But it was too late to back out now, right?

Chapter ⚬ Fourteen

was still in the shower when Simone arrived at my house the next morning. Bright and early. Unnaturally bright, actually (at least for Simone before noon on the weekend), and way too early (almost two and a half hours before I was supposed to meet Logan).

When I stepped into my room wrapped in a towel, Simone was hanging a garment bag from the curtain rod. A large, shiny purple case was sitting on my bed. I didn't have to look inside to know that it contained her entire makeup collection.

"Don't panic, I'm here," she sang out. "All ready to doll you up for your first date with Logan."

"It's not a date." I hesitated. "Necessarily."

She unzipped the garment bag. "Okay, I wasn't sure how dressy you wanted to get," she said. "I mean, it's a morning date, so you shouldn't look like you're trying too hard. But you want to look nice, right?"

"Right. That's why I was going to wear jeans and maybe my blue V-neck T-shirt." I walked over to my dresser and pulled out some clean underwear.

Simone looked dismayed. "The one you bought last month? No, I don't think so."

"What? Why not? You said I look great in that."

"For *school*." Simone shook her head. "You need something a little more special for a weekend date. Like this." She pulled a shiny purple minidress out of the bag with a flourish.

"You just said I shouldn't look like I'm trying too hard," I reminded her. "Besides, I'm going to the animal shelter, not dinner at the White House."

Simone chewed on her lower lip, turning the dress this way and that. "Maybe you're right—jeans should work fine with the right shirt." She hung the dress on the curtain rod beside the bag. "Maybe that black top with the sequins on the sleeves . . ."

As she dug through the garment bag, I quickly pulled on my underwear and dropped my damp towel in the hamper by the door. Even though Simone was acting kind of crazy, I was glad she was there. She was distracting me from being nervous. At least a little.

Every time I thought about meeting Logan, I felt a weird flip-flopping sensation in my gut. Was that the sparks at work again?

"This could work." Simone pulled out a bright pink shirt. "The color will look great on you, especially after I do your makeup. Here, try it on."

She tossed it to me, and I yanked it on over my head. "It's a little snug," I said, pulling at the front.

"No, it looks great! Hang on—I want to try something." She hurried over to the bed and snapped open her makeup case.

"Wait, what?" I watched as she started pulling out colorful tubes and bottles and vials. "Stop. What's wrong with my usual makeup routine?"

"Nothing—for school," Simone replied. "But you're not going to school today, remember? You're going on a date."

"It's not a—"

She didn't let me finish. "Don't worry, I know what I'm doing."

That was true. Simone had been going out on dates for years. Even if this wasn't a real date, it was still an outing with a guy friend, which was almost the same thing, right? Maybe she really did know best in this case. Or maybe I was still half-asleep and didn't feel like protesting. Either way, I was soon sitting cross-legged on my bedroom floor while she dabbed concealer onto my face.

As she worked, I tried to figure out what Logan had intended when he'd asked me to meet him at the shelter. Was it supposed to be a date? Simone seemed convinced it was, but I still wasn't sure.

Oh well. With any luck, I'd figure it out when I got there. I stifled a yawn as Simone used a giant brush to apply blush to my cheekbones.

"Hold still!" she ordered.

"Sorry. I didn't get to bed until late—our last customers were a bunch of hungry frat guys who didn't clear out until almost an hour past closing." I kept my face still, but slid my eyes toward her. "So what did you and Matt end up doing?"

"Dinner at the Chinese place on Oak. It was okay." She sat back to study my face. "Except we ended up spending like half the night talking about Ling and Megan's battle over Logan."

"Really?" I closed my left eye as she came at it with a tiny eyeshadow brush. "What did he say about it?"

"He thinks it's pathetic. Not that he'd ever say it to their faces."

"Can you blame him?" I opened my eye and looked at her. "Those two have really gone nuts over this. Like, scary psychokiller nuts."

Simone capped the mascara and tossed it back in her bag. "I know, right? They're acting like Logan's the last guy on earth or something." She leaned over, picking through the makeup bag. "Actually, though, I think it's just about the competition at this point. We all know they both hate to lose at anything. I bet that's the only reason neither of them will back down." She pulled out a tube of eyeliner and examined it. "It's not even about Logan himself anymore. I doubt they even really care about him."

I'd been thinking pretty much the same thing just the day before. Still, something about the way Simone was dismissing Logan's role in the whole thing rubbed me the wrong way. It wasn't as if two pretty, popular girls like Ling and Megan would make total fools of themselves over just anyone.

"I don't know about that," I told Simone. "Why *wouldn't* they care about him? He's a super-nice guy, and you said yourself he's cute."

She smirked at me. "Uh-oh, sorry—I didn't mean to insult Mr. Perfect," she said. "You're right, he's super droolworthy, and every girl wants him. There, is that better?"

I rolled my eyes. "Whatever. Are you done yet?"

"Not quite. Close your eyes and stop talking for a minute." She went back to work. "There," she said after a bit. "We can do your lips last. Now, about your hair—where's your curling iron?"

"No way." I put a protective hand to my head. "The last time I let you curl my hair, I ended up looking like Little Orphan Annie."

"Oh, please. We were like ten years old!" She fingered a strand of my damp, limp hair. "I just think you'd look cute with a few soft waves framing your face."

"Forget it." Climbing to my feet, I took a look at myself in the mirror. I was quite a sight. Simone had done an expert job on my eyes, giving them a smoky, almost exotic look. My lashes seemed a mile long, and my cheeks glowed with soft, sparkly pink blush.

"What do you think?" She hovered behind me, grinning like a loon. "Cute, right?"

"I don't know." I leaned closer for a better look. "I'm not sure Logan will even recognize me like this."

"Sure he will. Come on, at least let me help you dry your hair. Then you can finish getting dressed."

After one last glance at the semifamiliar face in the mirror, I followed her across the hall into the bathroom. It was still steamy from my shower, so I didn't have to look at my made-up face as I started blow-drying my hair. It was hard to miss that hot pink shirt, though. Even in the foggy mirror it glowed like a type II supernova.

"So what are you going to talk about on your date?" Simone asked, raising her voice to be heard over the roar of the blow-dryer.

"It's not a date," I replied, glad that my parents had already left for the restaurant. "And I'm guessing we'll mostly be talking about dogs."

"Okay. But you should have some other topics prepared just in case," she said. "Like current events, or funny stuff that happened in school, or . . ."

She babbled on for a while, but I wasn't paying much attention. When my hair was dry, I went back to my bedroom and pulled on my favorite jeans.

Then I looked in the mirror again. Simone's proud, smiling face appeared over my shoulder.

"You look perfect!" she exclaimed. "So adorable. Logan's going to love it."

I just stared at myself. At least I *thought* it was me. Between the makeup and Simone's pink shirt, I definitely didn't look much like my normal self.

Was that a bad thing? I wasn't sure. If Simone was right and this was supposed to be a date, maybe Logan would be expecting me to get all dressed up. Maybe he'd even be insulted if I didn't. On the other hand, what if he really did just want a friend's advice in choosing a dog? In that case, he was going to think I was insane if I showed up looking like this.

Besides, I wasn't that kind of girl. The kind who got all sparkly and fancy to try to win over a boy. Logan might as well know that from the start. Grabbing a tissue out of the box on my dresser, I glanced at Simone.

"Sorry," I said. "I appreciate the effort, but it's a little too much for me."

I wiped one eye, smearing glittery eye shadow across the tissue. "No!" Simone squawked, looking as stricken as if I'd just defaced the *Mona Lisa*. "But this is your first real date—I just want you to look as cute as you can."

"I know, and thanks. The trouble is, I don't look like *me*." I quickly wiped off the rest of the makeup. Then I pulled the pink shirt off over my head. "If this really is a date—"

"It is," she put in.

"Whatever." I handed her the shirt. "If it is, and if Logan really does like me as more than a friend—"

"He so totally does!"

"—then he'd better like the real me." I glanced at my naked face in the mirror. "Not some second-rate Simone clone."

Simone frowned for a second. Then she sighed. "Okay, fine,"

she said. "Natural girl it is. But you'll at least put on a *little* blush and eyeliner, right?"

Since my parents weren't home to drive me, I rode my bike to the animal shelter. The day was sunny but chilly, as if winter was digging its claws in, trying to hold on as long as possible. Logan was waiting outside the shelter when I got there. He smiled and waved as I pedaled over.

"Thanks for coming," he said, walking next to me as I wheeled my bike over to the rack. "I'm really excited about this!"

"Me too. It'll be fun." I quickly locked my bike, then straightened up. "Should we go in?"

"After you." He hurried over and opened the door, waiting for me to go through before him.

"Thanks." I shook off the chill as I stepped into the warm building. The sounds of muffled barking greeted us, along with the battling smells of animals and disinfectant.

The lady working at the desk was a regular Eats customer. "Bailey!" she greeted me. "So nice to see you. What can I do for you?"

I explained about Logan's quest. The woman nodded. "Yes, there was a note here about that when I came in this morning." She scrambled around on the messy desk. "The director said we could hold whichever dog you choose until next week."

She pointed us toward the dog section. Not that it would have been hard to find—most of the barking was coming from that direction.

"Let me know when you find one you like," the woman said. "I'll bring it to the meet-and-greet room so you can get to know it."

The dog room was noisy and active. Wire runs lined both walls of the long, narrow room, with a concrete aisle in between. In each cage was a dog, or sometimes more than one. For a few minutes we just walked around, peering in at each dog. Most of them seemed happy to see us, wagging their tails and sometimes barking or jumping up against the mesh fronts of the pens.

I paused to watch a pair of shepherd puppies wrestle. "So did you decide what kind of dog you want?" I asked as Logan stepped past me to the next run.

"I'm still not sure." He bent to let a medium-size hound type sniff his fingers through the wire. "I don't want anything too small and yappy, but Mom asked me not to get anything too huge, either."

"Okay. What else are you thinking?"

He shrugged. "I don't really know. I just figured a mutt is a mutt, you know?"

I glanced from a feisty little terrier barking nonstop in the next cage to the dog across the aisle, which appeared to be some kind of Lab mix. "Right, but you can guess at least a little about a dog's possible genotype from its phenotype."

"Uh-oh," he said. "You're talking science again, aren't you?"

"Oops." I shot him a sheepish look. "Sorry."

He reached over and poked me on the shoulder. "Just kidding," he said with a grin. "I love it when you talk science."

"Good. Because that's the only way I know how to talk, pretty much," I replied.

I was blushing a little, but there was none of the tongue-tied awkwardness that usually popped up at such moments. Come to think of it, being with Logan felt almost . . . easy. Like I really was just hanging out with a friend. A really, really cute and amazing friend.

"So, Professor," he said. "What's this genotype stuff you were talking about?"

"Oh, right." I stepped down the aisle to the next cage, where a tiny white dog peered up at me curiously. "I just meant that the way a dog looks can help you guess its breeding. So if you like, say, golden retrievers, you could see if any of the dogs have silky yellow fur or any other features that look like a golden. Because that might be a hint that they have some golden in them, which means a greater chance of them possibly having a similar type of personality."

"Gotcha." He stopped to look at the resident of the next run, a lean dog that appeared to be at least part greyhound. "I guess my mom's right and science really does make a difference in real life, huh?"

I grinned. "Definitely."

Just then a medium-size brown-and-white dog jumped up and barked at us from farther down the aisle, its fringed tail wagging furiously. "That one's cute," Logan said, hurrying over and offering his fingers for a sniff. "It looks sort of like a collie or something."

"He seems pretty friendly, too." I crouched down for a better look, and the dog examined me with a gaze so bright and curious that I couldn't help smiling.

"Yeah." Logan straightened up. "Think I should take this one to the meet-and-greet?"

"Definitely," I said, already heading for the door to summon the worker.

The meet-and-greet area was a small but cheerful room, with whitewashed cinder-block walls covered with colorful animal murals. There was a long wooden bench along one wall and several beanbag chairs scattered on the floor, along with numerous dog and cat toys.

"Cool place." Logan wandered around checking out the murals while we waited for the worker to bring the dog in.

"Yeah." I stared at a gaudy painting of a parrot. It reminded me of the makeup Simone had tried to make me wear.

The door opened and the worker came in with the brown-and-white dog on a leash. "Here you go," she said, handing the leash to Logan. "Let me know if you need anything. Otherwise, I'll leave you alone to get acquainted."

"Thanks." Logan bent down and held out his hand to the dog.

The dog sniffed his hand briefly, then dashed off to examine one of the toys on the floor, almost yanking the leash out of Logan's hand.

"I guess it's all right to let him loose, huh?" Logan said, reaching down to unsnap the leash from the dog's collar.

"I think so," I said.

I sat down in one of the beanbag chairs. Logan followed the dog around for a few seconds, then came over and flopped onto the chair beside mine.

"He seems kind of distracted," he said. "Maybe I should hang out and let him come to me when he's ready."

That didn't take long. The dog was eager to sniff everything he could reach, but soon he rushed back over to us, tail wagging nonstop. Logan grabbed a tennis ball and bounced it against the wall, and the dog raced after it and brought it back to him, looking proud of himself.

"Check it out," Logan said with a laugh. "I already taught him to fetch!"

"Either that or he already taught you to toss the ball for him," I teased.

"Works for me either way." Logan grinned and threw the ball again.

After that, Logan tried a few other toys. The dog was still a little distractible, occasionally rushing off to sniff the bench or the wall or whatever. But every time Logan snapped his fingers or whistled, the dog looked up alertly and then ran over to him.

"I think he likes me," Logan said with a laugh as the dog tried to crawl onto his lap.

"I think you're right." I reached over and scratched the dog behind the ears. "He's cute. Think he's the one?"

"I think so." His eyes met mine briefly, and he smiled. I held my breath, suddenly realizing how close we were to each other.

Then the dog leaped off Logan's lap, grabbed a rawhide bone, and started growling and shaking it furiously. That interrupted the moment, but I didn't mind. "This is fun," I said. "I'm glad I came."

"Me too. Otherwise I might never have found out what phenotype and genotype mean." From the sly little tilt of his mouth, I could tell he was joking around.

"Sure you would have," I retorted quickly. "I think we cover that in chapter seven or eight."

He laughed and reached down to pat the dog as it zipped past with the bone. I leaned back on my beanbag chair, feeling happy and comfortable. Okay, so maybe I still didn't know whether this was supposed to be a date or not. Either way, I really was glad I'd come. Being with Logan felt really . . . *right* somehow. Different. Special. Basically, sort of amazing.

As I was trying to figure out how I was going to describe it to Simone, the door swung open. I glanced over, expecting it to be the shelter worker coming to check on us.

But it wasn't her. Standing in the doorway, silhouetted by the morning sun coming in through the window behind the main desk, was a girl in a flirty green minidress, red hair flowing loose over her bare shoulders.

My jaw dropped. "Megan?" I blurted out.

"Hi, Bailey." Megan sashayed into the room, which suddenly felt a lot smaller with her in there. "Hey, Logan. What are you two doing here?"

I was wondering the same thing about her. Logan looked surprised too. He grabbed the dog as it darted toward the door, which Megan had left standing open behind her.

"I, uh, came to pick out a dog," he told Megan. "Bailey's helping me."

"Really? That's so weird—I'm thinking about adopting a dog too!" Megan clapped her hands, startling the dog into letting out a yip. "Crazy, huh?"

"Yeah. Crazy," I said, getting up to shut the door. This couldn't be a coincidence. Especially since I happened to know that Megan's younger brother was allergic to dogs.

"So who's this cute little guy?" Megan bent toward the dog, ruffling its ears. "Is this the one you're going to adopt, Logan?"

"I think so," Logan said, setting down the wiggling dog.

"What are you going to name him?" Megan smiled. "He looks like a Scamp. Or wait—maybe Joey?" She sat down in the spot beside Logan, the one I'd just vacated, pulling the dog toward her. "Here, Joey! Good boy!"

I perched on the end of the bench, feeling uncomfortable. How in the world had Megan figured out that Logan was at the animal shelter? Had he told her about it too—maybe even asked her along? He hadn't said anything about it to me. Then again, he wasn't exactly telling Megan to get out because we were on a date. . . .

Before I could figure it out, the door flew open again. "Logan! There you are!"

Ling? Seriously? Okay, now this situation was approaching an epic level of ridiculousness.

"Hi, everyone," Ling sang out as she hurried in. "What a coincidence! Looks like everyone's looking for a new dog today."

Megan glared at her. "Yeah, what a *coincidence*."

I glanced at Logan. He seemed confused as he looked from Megan to Ling and back again, not even noticing that the dog was gnawing on his shoelace.

Still, I couldn't help wondering if he'd known this might happen. How else would Megan and Ling both know they'd find him at the animal shelter, of all places? Maybe today wasn't as special as I'd started to think.

Ling sidled over to Logan, putting a hand on his arm. "So how long have you been here?" she asked.

"Umm . . ." Logan didn't seem to know what to say to that. He shot me a look. "A little while, I guess."

Suddenly I couldn't stand to be there for one more second. I jumped to my feet.

"I'd better get going," I said. "I need to go home and change before kickball."

"Really? Too bad." Ling didn't sound particularly disappointed. "See you, Bailey."

"Are you sure you have to go?" Logan asked.

"Yeah, sorry. But hey—mission accomplished, right?" I bent to give the dog a good-bye pat. His pink tongue darted out, slurping my hand.

I smiled. But the smile faded as I glanced at the other two girls, who were glaring at each other suspiciously. Yeah, it was time to get out of here. Past time, really.

As I hurried out the door, I comforted myself with one thought. At least I hadn't let Simone dress me up too much and curl my hair. Then I would have felt *really* stupid right now.

Chapter ● Fifteen

I wasn't really in the mood for kickball practice that afternoon, but I went anyway. I was still feeling kind of down after what had happened that morning, though I tried to tell myself that that was crazy—that I shouldn't have let myself get carried away in the first place.

But I couldn't help it. For a few minutes there, I'd really thought that Simone might be right. That maybe high school romance wasn't completely pointless. That Logan and I could be more than friends after all.

Stupid, stupid, stupid. What was I thinking, imagining I could compete with Megan and Ling? Why would I even want to try? That just wasn't me. I had a plan for my life, and this wasn't part of it.

The Lo-Ed team's practices always took place on the baseball diamond behind the high school. When I arrived, a bunch of people were already milling around out there, shouting and laughing loudly. The mood always got rowdier when there was a game coming up—especially the *big* game.

I was only halfway from the bike rack to the field when Simone came rushing toward me. She looked stricken. At first I assumed she was still upset about the whole animal-shelter fiasco. I'd told her all about it, of course. Mostly because she hadn't given me much choice. She'd been spying on my house from her window and had come rushing over as soon as I got home.

"Bailey, I'm so sorry," she exclaimed. "I just realized what happened this morning is all my fault!"

"No it isn't," I said. "No amount of makeup would have saved that sorry situation, trust me."

"Huh? No, not that." She waved a hand, shooing away my comment like a pesky fly. "The thing is, I realized there was only one other person who knew about your date. You know, besides you and me and Logan himself."

"And whoever Logan told," I added. "Which apparently included Ling and Megan."

"Not necessarily. See, I remembered that I told Matt while we were out last night. So I asked him just now if he told anybody else, and he said he mentioned it to Darius this morning while they were playing basketball. And Darius said he might have let something slip to Megan after that."

"Might have?" I glanced over at Darius and Matt, who

were kicking a ball around with some other guys out near second base.

"Yeah," Simone said. "Don't you get it? Logan didn't tell Megan about your date—*Darius* did. That's why she crashed."

"Why would Darius tell Megan something like that?"

"Who knows? Who cares? The important thing is, Logan didn't do it. He didn't want Megan and Ling there any more than you did."

"We don't know that." I was trying to take this in, work out the logic. "And speaking of Ling, how'd she find out about it? Darius didn't tell her, too, did he?"

"He said he didn't." Simone shrugged. "But who knows? Maybe Megan told her—the girl can't keep a secret to save her life. Or maybe Ling has some sort of superspy satellite system tracking Megan's every move, or Logan's. I wouldn't put it past her."

I actually cracked a smile at that. "Yeah, me neither."

She gripped my arm so tightly I was afraid it would leave a mark. "I feel so horrible about this, Bails!" she exclaimed. "I wanted you to have the most perfect date ever, and instead I totally ruined it. But don't worry, I already figured out how to make it up to you."

"You did?" I was instantly suspicious. "How?"

She grinned. "I invited Logan to kickball practice."

"What?" I blurted out.

"Yeah. He seemed really into it too. Come on, let's go say hi."

She dragged me off toward the field. For a second I was too

stunned to resist. "I can't believe you did this!" I hissed. "I don't need some stupid pity date. I'm going home."

"Too late—there he is. He already saw you." She dropped my arm and waved. "Hi, Logan! Over here!"

Logan separated from the mass of players over near the pitcher's mound. He waved, then loped toward us. He was wearing a T-shirt and a pair of baggy shorts. Even though I was seething with rage at Simone, I couldn't help noticing that Logan had nice legs—not too muscley, not too skinny.

"Hi, Bailey," he said when he reached us. "Listen, so I ended up reserving that dog. I think I'm going to call him Patch."

My first instinct was to ask if that name had been Ling's idea or Megan's. Instead I forced a smile.

"Sounds good," I said. "He seemed like a really nice dog."

"Yeah." Logan jammed his hands in his shorts pockets and stood there, rocking back and forth. There was a moment of awkward silence.

Simone glanced from me to Logan and back again, her happy expression fading into one of concern. Just then a piercing whistle came from the direction of the pitcher's mound. Simone glanced that way.

"Looks like we're getting started," she said. "We'd better get over there or Vinnie will pop a blood vessel."

I was grateful to her for ending the awkward moment, even though she was the one who'd caused it. We all headed for the pitcher's mound.

"Who's Vinnie?" Logan asked as we walked.

"Our coach," I said. "Tall skinny guy over there with the whistle."

Simone nodded. "He's a senior, so he's really determined to kick some Co-Ed butt this year," she told Logan. "Especially since the Lo-Ed team has lost the past two years."

Vinnie was standing in front of the dugout with a whistle hanging out of his mouth. Simone led us over to him.

"Hey, Vinnie, this is Logan," she said. "He wants to play. He just moved here."

Vinnie looked Logan up and down. "You any good?"

"Guess we'll find out," Logan replied with a shrug. "I haven't played kickball since I was a kid."

It turned out he *was* pretty good. Watching Logan kick and field and even pitch, I actually forgot about that morning's disaster. Mostly, anyway. By the end of practice, Vinnie was treating him like his new best friend. Everyone else seemed glad to have him on the team too.

"Welcome to the Lo-Eds, bro," Darius said, clapping Logan on the back as we all straggled off the field.

"Yeah," Zoe added. "Maybe we'll actually pull out a win this year."

"Hey, miracles happen, right?" Matt barked out a laugh, then bent down and wiped his sweaty face on Simone's shirtsleeve.

"Ew!" she cried, shoving him away. "You're such a dork!"

"I know. But you love it." He grabbed her by the waist and

twirled her around and around. She pretended to still be annoyed, but she couldn't help laughing.

"Knock it off, you two." Darius grabbed Matt's arm, making him stumble and almost drop Simone in the mud. "I'm starving. Who's up for pizza?"

"I've got a better idea." Simone shoved Matt away and reached back to adjust her ponytail. "Let's all go to Eats. I'm craving some hot chocolate."

Zoe's eyes lit up. "Excellent idea!"

Uh-oh. I shot Simone an irritated look. Was this another of her not-so-subtle attempts at shoving Logan and me together? Would that girl never learn?

Matt and Darius traded a glance and a shrug. "Come to think of it, I could go for a Belly Buster turkey platter," Darius said.

"Yeah." Matt glanced at Logan. "You in, bro?"

"Sure." Logan smiled at me. "Let's go."

What was I supposed to do now? Killing Simone was right up there on the list of possibilities, but instead I just smiled back at Logan.

"Um, sure," I said. "Sounds good."

Great-Aunt Ellen was behind the counter when we came in. She was tiny and plump and pink-cheeked, with purple-framed spectacles hanging on a chain around her neck and a crazy laugh that sounded like a dying foghorn. As I might have mentioned, she also baked the best cookies, cakes, and pastries in the world.

"Bailey!" she greeted me, her hazel eyes twinkling. "Come to work an extra shift?"

"No way, you can't have her!" Simone joked, wrapping her arms around me from behind. "She's off duty today."

"If you say so, Simone." Great-Aunt Ellen beamed at Simone. "Hello, Zoe. How are your parents?"

"They're fine," Zoe said. "They're still talking about that amazing cake you made for their anniversary."

"Good, good." Great-Aunt Ellen lifted her glasses to her face to peer curiously at the boys. "And who have we here?"

"This is my boyfriend, Matt," Simone said. "That's Darius, and that's Logan."

Just then Susannah bustled out of the kitchen carrying a tray of donuts. "Oh, hi, guys," she said. "What's up?"

"We just came from kickball practice," Matt told her. "We're pumped and ready to take you Co-Eds *down* next weekend!"

"Oh yeah?" Susannah smirked. "We'll see about that. Now, did you just come in here to trash-talk, or can I take your order?"

"Yes, what will it be, kids?" Great-Aunt Ellen said.

Simone glanced at the rest of us. "Hot chocolate all around?" she said.

"None for me," Logan said. "I'll just have a ginger ale or something."

Matt punched him lightly on the arm. "You'll regret that, Morse," he said. "The cocoa in this place is legendary."

"Can't do it, dude." Logan shrugged. "Allergies."

"You're allergic to hot chocolate?" Zoe sounded as horrified as if he'd said he was allergic to breathing. She wasn't as obsessed with all things *Theobroma cacao* as Ling was, but she came close.

"*Anything* chocolate," Logan clarified. "It's a bummer, but I'm used to it by now."

"Ginger ale it is." Great-Aunt Ellen made a note on her pad while Susannah headed for the soda machine along the back wall. "Anything else?"

Zoe and the guys ordered sandwiches, and Simone asked for one of the fresh donuts Susannah had just brought out. I passed on the solid food. Being around Logan made my stomach feel kind of funny, and I figured it was better not to risk it. I'd be lucky if I made it through this without spilling hot chocolate all over myself.

While Susannah took our order into the kitchen to make the sandwiches, we went to find a seat. All the booths were full, so we dragged two smaller tables together to make room for the six of us. I ended up sitting between Logan and Zoe. Across the table, Matt immediately threw one arm around Simone and started whispering in her ear, making her giggle. Zoe and Darius resumed the intense kickball strategy discussion they'd begun on the way over.

That left me and Logan. We listened to Zoe and Darius for a bit, but soon Logan started playing with the salt and pepper shakers. Uh-oh. Was he bored? Did he regret tagging along with us?

"Um . . . ," I began, trying to think of something to say.

He turned to me. "Did you say something?"

"No," I said. "I mean yes. Uh, so you're definitely getting that dog, huh? Um, Patch?"

"I think so." He looked worried. "Why? Do you think I shouldn't?"

"No, no, it's not that." Okay, I was really messing up here. Taking a deep breath, I eked out a smile. "I thought he was great. Really cute and fun."

"Oh. Good." He seemed relieved. "Because actually, after you left, Ling and Megan were both saying I shouldn't decide too quickly, before I checked out all my options. They dragged me back out to look at some other dogs."

"Really?" I was already regretting this. Why had I brought up our trip to the animal shelter, given how it had ended?

He nodded. "They both said they were looking for dogs too. But the funny thing is, they kept pointing out dogs they thought *I* should get. For instance, Megan insisted this one fluffy little Chihuahua cross would be perfect."

"Yeah, I don't really see you with a Chihuahua." I actually smiled as I tried to imagine it. "Did she want you to carry it around school in your backpack, like those celebrities who stick them in their purses?"

"Maybe." He laughed. "I told her I wanted a dog that could go running with me and stuff like that. So next she picked out a nice wiener dog with legs about two inches long, and Ling found this big black thing that was approximately the size of a small horse."

"Ling did take riding lessons for a while back in middle school," I said. "Maybe she thought it *was* a horse."

He laughed. "Anyway, after that Megan was trying to talk me into getting these two puppies that were barely old enough to have their eyes open. They were awfully cute, but I'm not sure I'm ready to raise two puppies. Not to mention what Mom would say."

"Did you tell Megan that?" I asked.

"Yeah. She said she was experienced with baby animals and was willing to come over a lot and help me. Ling seemed pretty skeptical, though. She said Megan's never even had a dog before." He shot me an amused look. "True?"

"True." I felt a little guilty blowing Megan's cover, but it sounded as if Ling had already taken care of that. "Her dad has an incredible saltwater fish tank in his dental office, though."

Logan nodded. "Good thing I didn't have those two helping me from the start. Otherwise I probably never would've found Patch." Leaning closer, he nudged me with his shoulder. "Thanks again for coming this morning."

"You're welcome. It was fun."

Just then Susannah arrived with our order. Zoe and Matt razzed her a little more about being on the Co-Ed team; Susannah threatened to take all their food back to the kitchen and spit in it; everyone cracked up. Good times. After that, everyone talked and laughed and ate, and Logan fit in so well that it was hard to remember he hadn't always hung out with us.

Later, after we'd finished every speck of food on the table,

Darius checked his watch. "Whoa—it's getting late. I'd better go," he said, sounding reluctant. "I'm supposed to babysit my little sisters tonight."

"On a Saturday night?" Matt shook his head. "Oh, dude!"

"Yeah. My parents have date night tonight." Darius made a face. "Lame, right? But hey!" He brightened. "You guys could come over if you want. We could play some video games, order a pizza . . ."

"Pizza?" Simone let out a groan. "How can you even think about eating again already?"

Matt ignored her. "I'm in," he said, standing up to trade a high five with Darius. Then he turned to Logan. "What do you say? D has a huge video-game collection."

"Really?" Logan looked interested. "Okay, sounds fun. I'm there."

Matt high-fived him, too. Then he reached down and tugged on Simone's ponytail. "What about you, babe? Want to come watch me humiliate these two at every game ever invented?"

"Sounds thrilling, but I'll pass." Simone rolled her eyes, then glanced at Logan. "Sorry you got roped into hanging with these geeks tonight, Logan. I hope you have more interesting plans for the rest of the weekend. Doing anything fun tomorrow?"

She sounded totally casual and innocent, but I knew better. I tossed her a warning look.

Which she completely ignored, of course. "Because if you don't have anything going on, you should stop by here again," she continued brightly. "On Sunday mornings, Bailey's great-aunt makes these huge bear claws that are absolutely scrumptious. And since Bailey's working, she can make sure you get one fresh out of the oven. Right, Bails?"

"Sounds great, but I'll have to take a rain check," Logan said. "My parents are dragging me to some distant relative's fiftieth-birthday barbecue tomorrow. I'll be gone all day."

"Oh." Simone sounded disappointed. "Too bad."

I couldn't help being disappointed too. Not that I'd expected to hang out with Logan again tomorrow or anything. Still.

The other guys were already heading for the door. Logan stood to follow.

"This was fun, everyone," he said, smiling at Simone and Zoe. Then he reached down and squeezed my shoulder. "See you on Monday, Bailey."

Simone smirked at that, and even Zoe raised an eyebrow. Luckily, Logan didn't notice, since he was already hurrying after the other guys.

My hand strayed to my shoulder where he'd touched it. "Yeah," I murmured, even though he was already too far away to hear me. "See you."

Chapter ● Sixteen

"Earth to Bailey." Susannah waved her hand in front of my face. "You there?"

I blinked and straightened up. The Sunday morning rush had petered out, and the brunch crowd wouldn't start trickling in for another hour or so. I was supposed to be changing the filters in the coffee machine. Now I realized I'd drifted off into a daydream partway through. I know it wasn't physiologically probable that my shoulder was still tingling where Logan had squeezed it the previous afternoon. But it felt as if it was.

"Sorry," I told Susannah. "What did you say?"

She grabbed the last filter out of my hand and slid it into place. "I said I'm going to make a delivery, and your dad's on the phone. Can you handle the register by yourself for a few minutes?"

I glanced out at the mostly empty tables. "I think I can manage," I said with a smile.

I was counting the change in Methuselah's drawer when Ling came in. I hadn't seen or spoken to her since leaving the animal shelter the day before.

"Bailey," she said briskly, hurrying over. "Good, you're here."

"Where else would I be? I'm always here," I joked weakly as I slid the cash drawer shut. "Want some coffee?"

"No, thanks." She leaned forward. "So is it true that Megan came in here the other day and bought some fancy personalized cupcake for Logan?"

"Um, where did you hear that?" Yes, I was stalling for time. Somehow it felt wrong to tattle on one of my friends to another. Even if they were both acting like huge idiots lately.

Ling smiled grimly. "Doesn't matter. Anyway, everyone knows she's being totally pathetic about this whole Logan thing."

I just cleared my throat. She seemed to take that as agreement.

"So I want to show Logan that I'm way cooler than her." Ling flipped her long, dark hair over her shoulder. "I'm going to get him a much better cupcake." She stepped over to peer into the bakery case. "Which kind did she give him?"

I still felt guilty for talking about Megan behind her back. Not to mention a little irritated by the way Ling was acting. But the scarily intense look in her eye made me afraid not to answer.

"The regular kind." I pointed. "Vanilla with buttercream frosting."

"Bo-ring!" Ling wrinkled her nose. "Seriously, the girl has *no* imagination." She leaned closer to the case. "What's that one? The big chocolate one there?"

"That's Great-Aunt Ellen's newest recipe—devil's food cake with triple-fudge frosting." Since none of us had known until the day before that Logan was allergic to chocolate, I guessed Ling didn't know it, either. "But—"

"That sounds amazing!" she interrupted, her eyes lighting up. "Can you put a message on that? And maybe some extra swirls or something to make it look fancier?"

"Sure, I guess. But listen—"

"How long will it take? I want to stop by his house as soon as it's ready." She leaned closer, glancing around to make sure nobody was listening. Since the only people in view were a couple of old ladies gossiping over tea and cookies, I wasn't sure why she was worried. "See, I'm hoping he'll decide to take me out to a movie or something. And the matinees all start before like one thirty."

"Okay. But seriously, Ling, I need to tell you something. . . ." Actually, a couple of things. Like that Logan would probably break out in hives if he even looked at that particular cupcake, and that he wasn't going to be home all day.

She looked up from digging through her purse. "By the way, I've been meaning to ask you." Her voice suddenly went sharp. "What were you doing with Logan at the shelter yesterday?"

I gulped. Was that suspicion I saw in her shrewd brown eyes?

"You don't have a little crush on him or something, do you, Bailey?" she demanded, leaning closer. "Because if you do, you'd better back off. It's annoying enough having Megan throwing herself at him without everyone else getting into the act."

I took a half step back, annoyance bubbling up inside me. Most of the time I liked to play it cool, avoid trouble. But this was too much. Sure, Ling could be kind of ruthless sometimes. But this was getting ridiculous even for her. What right did she have to tell me who I could or couldn't have a crush on?

"Don't be silly," I said as calmly as I could. "So you want the devil's food, huh? What's your message?"

She examined me for another second; then her face relaxed into a smile. "I just want it to say 'For Logan, from Ling.' Maybe in blue icing, if you've got some? That's his favorite color, you know."

"Blue it is." I scribbled the order onto the pad by the register. "It'll be ready in twenty minutes or so."

"Cool. That gives me just enough time to run to the drugstore and pick up some lip gloss. Just in case my lips get chapped from too much kissing or something, you know?" Ling pursed her lips playfully. "Be back in a few. Thanks, Bailey."

"No problem." I kept my smile steady until she was gone, then collapsed against the counter.

Had I really just done that? Wow. So not like me. Of course, there was no doubt Megan would have done what I'd just done, and worse, given the chance. Or Ling herself, for that matter.

Somehow, though, that didn't make me feel much better. Was I really turning into one of them?

I put my hand in the pocket of my apron, touching the smooth plastic casing of my cell phone. Maybe I should text Ling right now, tell her the truth. Well, the truth about Logan's chocolate allergy and his plans for today, anyway—I wasn't about to fill her in on my confusing and constantly changing feelings about Logan.

At that moment my father came through the swinging doors carrying a paper bag of sandwiches. "Bailey—just the person I wanted to see!" he sang out. "Want to run this delivery over to the dorms? It's a nice day out there—I figured you could use the fresh air."

"Sure. Is Great-Aunt Ellen still back there? We got a rush cupcake order." I ripped Ling's sheet off the pad and handed it to him. "She's coming back to pick it up in twenty minutes."

My dad nodded, and I made my escape with the sandwiches, telling myself it was no big deal. Logan wasn't home anyway, and Ling deserved a little payback for the way she'd been acting.

This didn't mean I was like her and Megan at all.

"The best part is, Ling totally blames Megan for the whole thing." Simone dodged a distracted freshman. "She thinks she set her up by talking about that cupcake she gave him."

We were on our way to last period. Simone was strolling along at her usual speed, but I kept catching myself wanting to hurry.

I'd spent the last two periods counting down the minutes until my study session with Logan. Pathetic, right? Especially since there was no decrease in Ling and Megan's craziness. If anything, they were getting worse. They'd pretty much monopolized his attention at lunch, leaving the rest of us talking among ourselves.

It didn't help that my bus had been even later than usual that morning, barely giving me the chance to say hi to Logan before the bell rang for homeroom. On top of that, Ms. Blumenkranz had jury duty this week, and the sub hadn't let us talk, or even do anything interesting. We'd spent art period reading about the history of impressionism in some dusty old textbooks she dug out of the back of the closet.

So basically, I'd only said about two words to Logan since Saturday. It shouldn't have mattered, but it did.

"So Ling actually lurked outside his house all day until he got home?" I asked as we turned the corner.

Simone nodded. "That's when she found out about his chocolate allergy."

"I still feel bad for not telling her about that." I smiled. "At least a little."

Simone shrugged. "You said you tried and she cut you off, right? No surprise there. She never listens when she's in that kind of mood."

She had a point. "So what did she do with the cupcake?"

"What do you think?" Simone laughed. "It was a chocolate cupcake with chocolate icing—of course she ate it herself!"

Logan hadn't arrived yet when we entered study hall. I felt a flutter of anticipation when I finally saw him step through the door.

"Here comes your boyfriend," Simone whispered.

"Shh! Don't call him that." I tried not to stare or blush or otherwise make an idiot out of myself as Logan walked toward us, smiling. Smiling at *me*.

My heart jumped. Okay, not really—that's physiologically impossible, of course. What actually happened was a rush of adrenaline, causing acceleration of heart and lung function, along with various other related symptoms. All of it caused by a release of chemicals in the brain.

Even though I had a pretty good intellectual understanding of my reaction, I was a little startled by it. What *was* it about Logan that did this to me every time?

"Hey," he said, dropping his backpack on the floor and sliding into his seat. "What's up? I feel like I've barely seen you today."

"Yeah." I busied myself with my backpack, not daring to meet his eye. "Ready to hit the books?"

"Sure." He bent down to grab his textbook out of his bag, and I caught myself admiring the way his bicep flexed as it moved.

Yikes. All along, I'd figured this would wear off eventually. But that wasn't happening. If anything, it was getting worse.

Logan sat up and opened his book. "Okay, you'll have to forgive me if I can't focus on this stuff too well today."

"Wh-what?" I tore my gaze away from his arm, feeling more than a little unfocused myself.

"Today's the big day, remember?" He grinned at me. "Dad's taking me to pick up Patch right after school."

"Oh! Right." I smiled back. "That's cool. You must be excited."

"Totally psyched. I made Mom and Dad stop at the mall on our way home yesterday so I could grab some dog food and a crate and a bunch of other stuff at the pet-supply store."

"Doggy shopping," I said. "Fun."

"Yeah." He flashed me a grin, then turned away and flipped open his textbook.

I stayed quiet, wondering if he'd mention finding Ling waiting for him when he got home. But he was scanning the table of contents.

"Where'd we leave off?" he asked.

"Chapter six," I reminded him. I slid my desk a little closer, trying not to notice how good he smelled as I scanned the textbook. "But first, maybe we should review what we went over on Friday."

"Good plan." He shot me a sidelong look. "I had a pretty exciting weekend—I may have forgotten everything you taught me."

The first thing that jumped into my mind was Ling again. Was he talking about finding her waiting for him at his house? Somehow I didn't think so. Apparently my cardiovascular system didn't think so either, since my heart was thumping along at double time again.

"Um, really?" I said.

"Nah, just kidding." Logan smiled at me. "You're a good teacher. I think I remember most of it."

"Oh. Um, good."

He glanced at the textbook, then back at me again, his expression suddenly turning more serious. "I really appreciate this, you know. Not just anybody would give up all their study halls for something like this."

"It's okay, I don't mind." I smiled tentatively. "I'm a science geek, remember? This is actually fun for me."

He grinned, looking relieved. "Cool. Still—thanks."

"You're welcome." I smiled back. If nothing else, we were kind of starting to feel like friends. Real friends. Maybe I should be grateful for that; maybe it was enough.

"Okay, so let's start our review . . . ," I began. Logan scooted his desk even closer to mine, and I tried not to notice how close his arm was to brushing against mine. That adrenaline was kicking in again, making me feel short of breath.

I was an evidence-based kind of girl, and the evidence seemed to be mounting, all of it pointing to one theory. That maybe being friends *wasn't* enough.

Chapter 🙾 Seventeen

When the bell rang to end bio class on Thursday, Mr. Ba asked Logan to stay after class.

"Just for a moment," the teacher assured Logan. "I want to go over the homework you turned in yesterday."

"Okay, sure." Logan sounded nervous. He turned around and shot me a questioning look.

"Don't worry, I'm sure you're fine," I said as I gathered my books. "You're making tons of progress in our study sessions. Mr. Ba probably just wants to check in and make sure you're understanding everything."

"You think so?" He still seemed nervous, but he gave me a small smile. "Thanks. I'll see you at lunch in a few."

"Okay."

I went over and waited for Simone, Megan, and Taylor by the door. Logan walked up to the teacher's desk. He still looked anxious, but I wasn't worried. We really had accomplished a lot on Monday and Wednesday afternoons. I might be clueless when it came to figuring out boys, but I knew I gave good bio tutoring.

When they reached me, Simone and the others were complaining about the homework Mr. Ba had just assigned. Simone stopped when she noticed me watching Logan.

"What's going on?" she asked.

"Nothing." I definitely didn't want to get into it in front of Megan. "Let's go, I'm starved."

Fortunately, she seemed to understand. She nodded, giving me a look that said, *We'll discuss later.*

Megan headed straight to our table while Simone, Taylor, and I went through the lunch line. When we emerged with our trays, I could see from halfway across the cafeteria that Matt and Darius weren't sitting with us today. Too bad. Just having a guy or two around tended to tamp down Ling and Megan's antics. At least a little.

"So I can't believe how sweet and shy Logan is," Ling was telling Zoe when we got close enough to hear. "When I asked to borrow a pen in English, he totally blushed when our hands touched."

Zoe sort of grunted, not looking up from her salad. Beside me, Simone let out a soft snort.

"Yeah, right," Megan said. "He's probably just embarrassed by how you're always pawing at him."

"Pot, meet kettle," Simone whispered, making Taylor cover her mouth to keep from laughing.

Ling heard them and looked up. "Oh, hi," she said, peering over our shoulders. "Where's Logan? Didn't he walk with you guys?"

"Had to stay behind and talk to the teacher." Simone dropped her bag lunch on the table. "Who knows, he might have to miss the entire lunch period."

"What?" Megan and Ling squawked in unison.

Taylor looked amused. "Relax, she's just messing with you. He'll probably be here soon."

"Whatever." Megan turned to Ling. "Anyway, like I was saying, you really need to back off. Everyone in school is talking about how desperate you look throwing yourself at Logan."

"*Me* back off?" Ling said. "How about *you* back off? Like this morning, when he so obviously wanted to talk to me about this weird dream I had, except you kept butting in."

"Get real." Megan's eyes rolled so dramatically I was afraid they'd get lost somewhere up in her skull. "Nobody wants to talk to you about your stupid dreams. He was totally making eye contact with me the whole time."

Ling just snorted. "Please."

Suddenly Zoe slammed her soda down so hard it made everyone else's lunches jump. "You know what? This is getting *really* old."

Everyone turned to stare at her, including me. Zoe was super competitive on the athletic field, but the rest of the time she was just about the most laid-back person I knew. If Ling and Megan were getting on *her* nerves, it had to be bad.

"What's with you, Zoe?" Ling asked.

"I'll tell you what." Zoe glared at Megan and Ling in turn. "You two seriously need to settle this Logan thing. Like, soon. Before you drive all of us crazy."

"She has a point, you guys," Taylor added tentatively. "You have been a little, like, intense lately."

Megan flipped her hair back. "It's not my fault she's trying to horn in on my guy."

"He's not your guy," Ling retorted. "If you weren't so delusional, you'd be able to tell he's into me."

"Enough!" Zoe cried so loudly that she drew curious glances from nearby tables. "Don't you even care that you're acting like total jerks to each other? You're supposed to be friends!"

Megan frowned for a second, then looked slightly chastised. "Okay, I guess I see your point." She glanced at Ling. "Maybe it's time to deal with this."

"Maybe." Ling shrugged. "Logan does need to make up his mind already."

"We should tell him that," Megan said. "I don't want to do it at school, though."

"Agreed." Ling wrinkled her nose as she looked around the cafeteria. "It'll have to be this weekend."

"How about talking to him at the kickball game?" Taylor suggested. "You'll all be there anyway."

"Good idea," Ling said, and Megan nodded.

"But don't do it right before the game, okay?" Zoe put in hastily, already sounding more like her usual self again. "Logan's one of our best players, and we can't afford to have you guys freak him out and make him choke."

"Fine, *after* the game." Ling already sounded bored of the whole topic. "Megan and I will pull him aside and confront him, make him decide which of us he wants to be with."

"What if he doesn't want either of you?" Simone said, a mischievous gleam in her eye.

I kicked her under the table. This situation was messed up enough without her dragging me into it. Which I could tell she was about to do.

Luckily, the others seemed to take the comment as a joke. "Very funny," Ling said, while Megan stuck out her tongue at Simone.

"Shh!" Taylor nodded toward the door. "Here he comes."

We all turned to watch Logan hurry toward us. He looked pretty happy, so I guessed the meeting with Mr. Ba had gone well.

"Hi, Logan!" Megan sang out, at the same time Ling said, "Come sit by me, Logan!"

"Hey, guys," Logan greeted the table at large. Ignoring Ling's command, he slid into the empty seat beside mine. "So guess what?" he told me. "Mr. Ba says I'm making tons of progress already—more than he expected."

"Really? That's amazing!" For a moment I actually forgot about the others. I was really happy for Logan. He'd been so worried that he couldn't handle the course, but I'd known all along that he could.

"I couldn't do it without you." He sounded so happy he was almost breathless. I wondered if he'd run the whole way from the science wing. "Mr. Ba pretty much came out and said I'm lucky to have someone like you who's willing to tutor me."

"Yeah, Bailey's a genius when it comes to sciencey stuff," Simone put in. "We'd all probably be flunking out of that class without her."

Logan flashed her a quick smile, then turned his attention back to me. "So anyway, I wanted to figure out a way to thank you." He glanced down and started unwrapping his sandwich. "I was thinking the least I could do is maybe buy you a slice of pizza or something. What do you say? Are you free after school?"

Simone let out a tiny gasp. Everyone else went silent for a moment. The entire cafeteria seemed to be holding its breath. Or maybe that was just me. I was stunned, but not in a bad way. This time there was no mistaking it. He'd just asked me out—right?

I knew what I had to do. I knew what I *wanted* to do. Feeling suddenly bold, I opened my mouth to accept his invitation.

Before I could get the words out, Ling jumped in. "Oh,

Bailey can't do anything after school," she said, leaning across the table. "She has to work at the restaurant. Every day."

That wasn't true, and everyone at the table knew it. Everyone except Logan, that is. His face fell.

"Really?" he said.

"Yeah," Megan jumped in. "Plus Bailey hates pizza."

Also not true. Which Megan knew.

"But I *love* pizza," Megan went on. "There's this awesome place over on Jackson Street—I could show you this afternoon if you want."

"No way," Ling put in quickly. "Everyone knows the pizza at Romano's is way better." She turned to Logan. "What do you think? Want to check it out after school?"

"Um . . ." Logan didn't seem to know what to say.

I didn't know what to say either. Were my so-called friends really doing this? Shoving me aside, not even noticing that I might like this guy too? Or maybe just not caring?

"Bails?" Simone whispered, leaning closer with concern in her eyes. "You okay? Want me to say something?"

"No!" I whispered. I stood up, raising my voice so the rest of the table could hear. Not that any of them were listening. "I'm going to grab more napkins."

Not bothering to wait for a response, I hurried away.

I was still in a funk on Friday afternoon. Even learning that neither Megan nor Ling had succeeded in wrangling Logan into taking them out for pizza the day before hadn't cheered me up much.

After thinking about it all day, I thought I knew why. If the feelings between me and Logan were as real as I'd been starting to think—as real as Simone kept insisting they were—shouldn't this be easy? Or at least not quite so awkward and complicated?

For once, I was almost dreading study hall. When Simone and I walked in, Logan was already in his seat.

"Smile," Simone hissed in my ear as we headed toward him. "He asked you out once, remember? Possibly twice. And it's almost the weekend now. Maybe he'll try again."

"Shh!" The girl was nothing if not persistent. She'd been giving me pep talks for the past twenty-four hours straight.

Logan glanced up from his bio book when he heard us coming. "Hey!" he said, breaking into a big smile. "How was English? Did you do all right on your quiz?"

For a second I was confused. How did he know I'd had a quiz in English today? Then I remembered talking to Simone and Zoe about it at lunch that day. I'd thought Logan was distracted by Megan and Ling yammering at him from both sides, but maybe he'd heard me after all.

"Oh," I said. "I think I did okay. Thanks."

Simone was still standing in the aisle. She cleared her throat. "So listen, Bailey," she said loudly. "I can't hang out with you after school today after all. I just remembered I have a dentist appointment."

"What?" I had no idea what she was talking about. For one thing, we hadn't discussed hanging out after school. For another, she'd just been to the dentist like two weeks earlier.

"Sorry to bag out on you." Simone shrugged. "I guess you'll have to find something else to do, since you don't have to work today." She glanced toward the classroom door. "Oh, look, there's Taylor. I'll leave you guys to your studying." With a quick wave, she rushed off.

Now I got it. At least she hadn't poked Logan in the shoulder and said, "Hint, hint!" at the end. I supposed I should be grateful for small favors.

"So you're off work today, huh?" Logan said as I sank into my seat. "I thought Ling said you had to work every day after school."

"Not every day." I unzipped my bag. "It just seems like every day sometimes. That's probably what she meant." Okay, or maybe not. What Logan didn't know wouldn't hurt him.

"Cool. In that case, I have an idea."

"Um, what?" I couldn't believe it. Was he actually taking Simone's bait?

He grinned. "Patch is cool, but he's pretty hyper. I was thinking of taking him over to campus for a good run this afternoon. Want to come?"

I hesitated. Was this a pity date? Or was he still feeling indebted to me because of the tutoring thing? Or what?

But suddenly it didn't matter. I was a scientist—I liked to know things. And right then what I needed to know was what the deal was with my feelings for Logan. This was my chance to gather a little more evidence one way or the other.

So what if it wasn't easy? Since when did that scare me off? Everything in biology was complicated—I lived for complication! As for Megan and Ling? Yeah, they were definitely two *big* complications. But I'd just have to deal with any fallout from that direction later.

"Sure," I told Logan before I could change my mind. "Sounds fun—I'm in."

Chapter ☾ Eighteen

Before leaving study hall, Logan and I arranged to meet up on campus an hour after the final bell. That would give him time to go get Patch, and me time to drop off my books at home.

It seemed like a perfectly logical plan. But by the time I got off the bus in front of my house, I was freaking out. I wasn't like Simone or the others. I just wasn't cut out for this boy-girl stuff. I should have stuck to my plans to avoid high school romance.

"What was I thinking?" I muttered as I pushed through the front door and stomped toward the stairs. "For a smart girl, I sure am an idiot sometimes."

"Bailey? Is that you?"

It was my mother. She wandered out of the kitchen holding a coffee mug.

I pasted a bland smile on my face. "Hi, Mom," I said. "I thought you'd be at work."

"I'm waiting for your sister." She took a sip of coffee. "She's got gymnastics today. Besides, I told your dad I'd take the late shift tonight so he and Uncle Rick can go to the Spring Thing lacrosse game."

"Oh." I wasn't really listening. "That's cool. I mean, whatever."

Mom was watching me carefully. "You okay, Bailey? You seem a little agitated. Did you have trouble with that English quiz?"

"No, quiz was fine. All my classes were fine."

"What, then?" She took my arm and steered me into the kitchen. "Is anything wrong? You can talk to me."

"I know, Mom. And seriously, nothing's wrong." I glanced at the clock on the microwave. Fifteen minutes before I needed to leave. "Hey, Mom, can I ask you something?"

"Anything," she said immediately.

I perched on the edge of one of the bar stools at the kitchen island. "When did you know that Dad was the guy for you?"

She looked a little surprised. No wonder. I couldn't remember the last time I'd asked her a question like that. Probably because there wasn't a last time.

"Hmm, I don't know if I could pinpoint the exact time." She leaned against the counter across from me. "We've known each other since we were kids. Is there a reason you're asking this right now?"

"Sort of." I took a deep breath. "See, there's this guy . . ."

"A guy?" She perked up in a very Simone-like way.

"Relax," I said quickly. "I haven't decided what to do about him yet. It's just—I never thought I'd like a guy in high school, you know?"

"But you like this guy?"

"Maybe." I considered. "I mean, yes. Probably."

"Wow!" Mom caught herself. "Er, I mean, go on."

I couldn't blame her for the reaction. She'd probably been wondering when I was going to get with the program, start acting like a typical hormonal teenager. "It's just, this wasn't part of the plan, you know?" I said. "I wasn't going to let myself get distracted by this kind of stuff."

"It doesn't have to be a distraction." She smiled. "At least not a bad one."

"Right, easy to say that now." I clutched the edge of the countertop. "But what if things work out with him and I end up letting my grades slip? I could be kissing my MIT acceptance good-bye!" Noticing my mother's mouth twisting in a strange way, I peered at her suspiciously. "Mom? This isn't funny!"

"I know. I'm sorry." She arranged her features into a more somber expression. "I just don't know too many high school sophomores who are so concerned about getting into the college of their choice that they see dating as a distraction."

She was just noticing this now? "I know, I'm a freak," I muttered.

"No, you're not, sweetie." She reached across the counter and squeezed my hand. "You're unique, but that's okay. It's part of what makes you lovable."

I squeezed back, then let go and started picking at my fingernails. "So what am I supposed to do?"

"I can't tell you that, Bailey." Mom sipped her coffee, watching me over the rim of the mug. "What I *can* say is that while it's good to have a plan, you have to stay flexible. You can't count on things working out exactly like you think they will."

"What do you mean?"

"Well, just look at Simone's mom. When we were your age, she was fully planning to marry her high school boyfriend as soon as possible—that would be Ray Baird from the auto shop."

"Simone's mom went out with *Mr. Baird*?" That was a shock. Mr. Baird was nice enough, I supposed, but he was bald and paunchy and always smelled like gasoline. I didn't even know he was the same age as my mom and Mrs. Amrou—he seemed a lot older.

"That's right." Mom looked amused by my reaction. "The two of them were going to buy into College Avenue Eats once Celia and I got out of college, and all of us were going to work together. Along with your dad, of course."

"Wow." I couldn't picture it. Simone's mom becoming Mrs. Baird and spending her days covered in flour and powdered sugar? Mr. Baird making sandwiches and chatting with customers?

"But then Celia went away to college, Ray met someone else, and the rest was history. Change of plans." Mom stood and went to the coffee pot to top off her mug. "And then there's me."

"What about you?" I asked. "You followed your plan, right? You married Dad, then went into the family business."

"Yes, that part worked out." Mom's smile turned kind of wistful around the edges. "But I always thought I'd have a whole passel of kids. In the end, though, I only ended up being able to have you two girls."

"Really?" I hadn't known that. It gave me a weird feeling to hear it, actually. What else didn't I know about my own mother?

"Uh-huh." Mom stared into her mug. "Then there's Susannah. She wanted to be a nurse from the time she was a little girl."

I remembered that. "She used to pretend my stuffed animals were her patients. And she cleaned and bandaged my scratches and scrapes that time I fell out of the tree house."

"And yet here she is, taking business classes. Seems like a change of plans, doesn't it?"

I frowned. "Sure, but I thought she decided she'd rather study business so she could take over Eats someday."

Mom shrugged. "That's what she says now. But I suspect she felt obligated to make that decision—she's Rick and Vera's only child, after all. And she's always been the type of person who hates disappointing anyone."

"Wow." I thought about all the times Susannah complained about her business classes. Was she secretly dreaming of taking pharmacology and anatomy instead of finance and accounting?

"Anyway, I'm glad you're not like that, Bailey." Mom smiled

at me. "I admire the way you're so determined to follow your dreams."

"Oh." I'd never really thought about it that way. Here I'd figured I was just sort of stubborn. "Thanks, Mom."

"I mean it, sweetie." She was giving me one of those doting Mom smiles, the kind I usually rolled my eyes at but secretly sort of loved. "I hope you'll be that way about everything in life. I hope you'll never back down or give up on something you really want."

I just nodded, my mind wandering back to Logan. Was that what Mom was talking about? Did she want me to go for it?

That reminded me to check the time again. "Oops, I'd better go." I slid off the stool and headed toward the door. Then I turned back and hurried around the counter to give her a quick hug. "Thanks, Mom. I mean it."

It was the first day of the Spring Thing, and the entire campus was buzzing with energy. The school colors were everywhere—on the Spring Thing banners that flapped in the breeze on every lamppost and building and on the T-shirts and hats of students wandering around. I strolled through campus, enjoying the festive mood and the warm, breezy afternoon. There was an informal soccer game going on in front of University Hall, and I could hear the faint sounds of a band playing somewhere in the distance.

Logan and I had arranged to meet by the benches on the east end of Campus Lawn, a big parklike area between the main part of campus and the outer dorms. It was always a popular spot for jogging, sunbathing, walking dogs, or just hanging out. Today it actually looked a little less crowded than usual, probably because so many people were over enjoying the activities on Main Campus.

Hearing a bark, I turned and saw Logan jogging toward me with his new dog pulling him along. "Sorry I'm late!" Logan called breathlessly. "Believe it or not, Dad had Patch out for a walk when I got home, and I had to wait for them to get back."

"It's okay, I just got here." I bent to pet Patch, who jumped up and licked my face, his tail wagging so fast it was a blur. "I hope he's not all worn out from his walk."

"No way." Logan laughed. "Trust me, nothing wears this guy out!"

I noticed he had his backpack on, and something was sticking out the top. "What's that?"

"Oh! Check it out. Here, can you hold him for a sec?" Logan handed me Patch's leash, then took off his backpack. "It's a kite—see? Since it's kind of windy today, I thought we could try it. If you want?"

"Sure!" I had to smile at his eagerness. "I can't remember the last time I flew a kite."

"Really? I love kites." As he talked, Logan was expertly unfurling the kite. It was a good-size one, diamond-shaped with multicolored fabric stretched across a wooden frame. "I got really into it when I lived in California. One of my mom's colleagues there belonged to the local kite club and he used to let me tag along to their events."

"Sounds fun." I'd never met a guy who was interested in kites before. Then again, I'd never met anyone like Logan before. "So what do we do?"

I took a step closer. Patch had been staring at a squirrel rustling around in a tree nearby, but now he focused on the kite. With a bark, he pounced on its fluttering tail.

"Patch, no!" Logan yanked the tail loose. "Bad dog!"

Patch tilted his head and stared at him, tail wagging slowly. Then he barked and leaped to the end of his leash, almost yanking it out of my hand as another squirrel scurried by.

Logan sighed and grinned at me. "This could be more challenging than I thought."

I giggled, taking a tighter grip on the leash. "I love a challenge!"

Soon Logan had the kite ready to go. I held Patch a safe distance away, watching as Logan dashed across the grass, letting the string feed out behind him. Things started pretty well—the kite rose steadily into the sky, its tail fluttering—but then a stray breeze sent it off course.

"Oh, no!" Logan yelled, running even faster as the kite wobbled and dipped.

It was no use. The kite plummeted to the earth, top first, and embedded itself in the soft soil of the green. Several college students lounging nearby whooped and applauded, and Logan took a sheepish bow.

I caught up to him just as he'd finished rerolling the string onto the reel. Patch was frisking at my feet, nipping at the grass.

"Hey, it looked pretty good there for a minute," I said with a smile.

"Thanks. Want to give it a try? I can take Patch."

"Sure."

My turn didn't go any better than his, at least at first. For one thing, Logan kept coming closer to give me advice on how to hold the kite and which direction the wind was blowing and stuff like that. It was pretty helpful, except that Patch kept trying to jump up and attack the kite.

After the third time the playful dog caught the kite's tail in his mouth, Logan wrestled him to the ground and laughed helplessly. "I guess maybe dogs and kites don't mix as well as I'd hoped," he said. "Sorry."

"No, it's okay. This is fun!" I meant it too. I was out of breath and I had the sneaking feeling those college students were laughing at us, but I didn't care.

"You sure?" He actually looked worried.

I smiled and nodded. "Positive. Now stand back—I'm going to get it up there next time no matter what!"

Okay, so it didn't happen the very next time. But on the try after that, I actually managed to get the kite to catch the breeze. I was so surprised when I saw it rising up behind me that I slowed down.

"Run! Run!" Logan shouted, sprinting toward me with Patch bounding along beside him. "You've got it—keep going!"

I picked up the pace again, running across the wide green

expanse of Campus Lawn as fast as I could. When I glanced back again, the kite looked a little wobbly. But it was still rising.

Logan and Patch caught up to me. The dog barked and leaped, and Logan shot me a thumbs-up with his free hand. "You've almost got it!" he called.

I nodded and pumped my legs harder. A moment later I felt a funny sort of tug on the reel I was holding, then a steady pull on the line.

"You got it!" Logan cried. "You can stop now—check it out!"

I stopped and turned around, looking for the kite. Up, up, up . . . My jaw dropped as I saw how high it was.

"I did it!" I could hardly believe it. "Look at that!"

The kite soared, seeming almost as high as the wispy clouds floating across the bright blue spring sky. I held tightly to the reel, afraid that if I let go the kite would fly off to the moon. Even though I knew that was impossible—for one thing, it would never be able to achieve escape velocity. . . .

"Patch, no!" I exclaimed as the dog jumped up on me, trying to reach the little bit of line hanging down from the reel.

"Easy, boy." Logan pulled him away. "Good job, Bailey. So what do you think?"

I glanced at him and grinned. "I think I'm a kite-flying genius, that's what I think."

He laughed. "Why am I not surprised you're good at this? It's lucky I'm not an insecure kind of guy or I'd be totally intimidated by your awesomeness."

I blushed, even though I was pretty sure he was just kidding around. Suddenly I felt a drop in the tension on the line. I glanced up. The kite was lower than it had been a few seconds ago.

"Hey, what's happening?" I tugged at the line.

He looked up too. "Reel it in a little and start moving—see if you can settle it again."

No dice. Within seconds the kite was falling fast.

"Run!" Logan urged. "Hurry—it's coming down!"

I took off with Logan and Patch beside me. We were running out of space—if I kept going that way, I'd run smack into the side of the university's student center. "What now?" I yelled.

"Turn around and run even faster! And reel in! You've got to head it off!"

I shot him a look of disbelief. Run faster? He had to be kidding.

But I did it—or tried to, anyway. Veering around, I sprinted back across the green, faster and faster . . .

THUMP!

"Stop!" Logan yelled. "It's down."

I skidded to a halt and collapsed on the grass, completely out of breath. "Thank goodness," I gasped. "I couldn't take much more of that!"

Logan jogged over. Patch pricked his ears when he saw me lying down, then took a flying leap onto my stomach.

"Oof!" I grunted. "Patch, no!"

The dog ignored me, clambering across my chest and eagerly licking my chin. I pushed him away and sat up.

Logan collapsed beside me, grinning. "Sorry about that—he's a little too friendly for his own good."

"No, it's okay." I gave Patch a pat as Logan pulled him off me. Then I glanced at the kite, which was once again sticking out of the ground at an awkward angle. "Should I go get it while you roll up the string?"

"In a minute. I need to catch my breath first. You run pretty fast for a girl."

"Hey!" I shoved him, pretending to be insulted. "Girls can run. Besides, Vinnie has been whipping us into shape all season to run the bases faster."

"Well, it worked." He leaned closer, resting his shoulder against mine. "You ran me into the ground. And Patch, too."

All too aware of the sudden weight and warmth of Logan's shoulder, I glanced at the dog. Patch finally seemed to be tired. He'd just collapsed on the grass at Logan's feet, resting his head on his paws.

"Guess we finally wore him out," I said. "That's what we're here for, right?"

He didn't answer at first. Just leaned against me, still breathing hard.

I wanted to turn my head to look at him, but I didn't quite dare. He was so close. I could feel his warmth through our shirts, feel the rhythm of his breathing.

Then I felt him shift as he turned to face me. His shoulder pulled away from mine, but now our legs were touching. And Logan's face was only about six inches from mine.

"This is fun," he said softly. "I'm glad you came."

"Me too." Swallowing hard, I turned to face him. His eyes were so blue, especially this close.

He licked his lips, looking nervous. I held my breath as he leaned forward . . .

A flurry of barking exploded at our feet. "Patch!" Logan blurted out as the leash slipped from his hand. "No!"

The dog ignored him, running off at top speed after a squirrel. Logan scrambled to his feet.

"We've got to catch him," he cried. "He's not supposed to be off leash here!"

I followed as he raced after the dog. "Patch, stop! Come! Sit!" I yelled.

Patch ignored me, totally focused on his quarry. The squirrel headed straight up the nearest tree, leaving the dog barking wildly at the bottom.

"Need some help?" called out a cute college guy with floppy hair.

"I think I've got it," Logan called back breathlessly, making a dive for the end of Patch's leash.

But the dog was too quick for him as he made a quick dash across the grass.

"Patch!" I hollered after him.

Realizing we were facing a losing battle, the floppy-haired guy tried to grab him, but Patch darted to the side and barked, his tail wagging even harder. He seemed to think we were all playing an awesome game of tag.

By then more students were running over to help. For the next few minutes Patch led us all on a merry chase, obviously delighted to be loose and the center of attention. Finally a college girl used a granola bar to lure him close enough to grab the leash, and the great escape was over.

"Thanks." Logan looked sheepish as he accepted the leash from the college girl. "Sorry about that."

"No worries." She leaned down and ruffled Patch's ears, then offered him half the granola bar, which he slurped up eagerly. "I won't turn this little guy in to the campus cops."

Everyone laughed, including me. But I couldn't help being disappointed. Whatever that moment had been between Logan and me, it was over now.

If only that squirrel hadn't come along at just the wrong time . . .

Chapter ● Nineteen

D o you really think he was going to kiss you?" Simone asked eagerly.

I shot her a look. "How many times do I have to tell you? I don't know." I paused, thinking back to the previous afternoon. "It really kind of felt like that, though. Not that I know what that feels like. You know."

She nodded and squeezed my arm. It was Saturday, and we were walking across campus toward the athletic fields, where the kickball championship was due to start in less than half an hour. Simone's dad had just dropped us off on College Avenue. I hadn't wanted to discuss my love life in front of him, of course, which meant this was my first chance to talk to Simone about Logan since last night, when I'd called to give her the full report.

"So how did you leave things?" Simone asked. "After the squirrel incident, I mean."

I shrugged. "I already told you. We rolled up the kite string, then walked Patch a little more. Then it was getting late and Logan said he had to get home for dinner. He walked me to Eats and said good-bye. . . ."

"No kissing attempt then?" Simone looked hopeful, as if she actually thought I might have been keeping that kind of juicy tidbit a secret.

"No. He left to walk to his house, and I went inside and talked Aunt Vera into giving me a lift home. The end."

Ahead, I could hear the sounds of shouts and laughter and general ruckus. We were nearing the university baseball field that would be the site of the kickball showdown of the century. Or at least of this spring.

"No kiss," Simone mused. She shrugged. "Still, I think it counts as a date. I wonder what he'll do when he sees you today?"

I was wondering the same thing. Part of me was excited to see him again. Another part was terrified. Megan and Ling would both be at the game today—they always came to cheer on the Lo-Ed team. Would they notice that things were different between Logan and me?

Were things different between Logan and me?

I supposed I was about to find out, since we were almost to the field. As usual, the scene was total pandemonium. The bleachers along the first-base line and behind the dugout were overflowing with spectators. I spotted a bunch of people I knew from school, including a few teachers.

The high school team was warming up with some kicking drills, while the college kids were just hanging out near home plate. I waved to Susannah, who was chugging a sports drink and chatting with her boyfriend. She waved back, but Chuck and several of her other teammates grabbed her and forced her arm down, yelling something about fraternizing with the enemy. Susannah giggled and raised her hands in surrender.

Then I heard someone calling my name. Gabi and Gwen were hurrying toward us. "Hey, you guys came!" I exclaimed.

"Nice T-shirt," Simone added with a laugh.

Gwen was dressed all in black, as usual, but Gabi was sporting a homemade T-shirt with CRUSH THE CO-ED CRAZIES! written on it in neon fabric paint.

"Very creative," I told Gabi. "Obviously Ms. Blumenkranz is rubbing off on you."

She grinned. "What can I say? I have the soul of an *artiste*. Anyway, we're psyched to see you guys crush the Co-Eds, right, Gwen?"

Gwen rolled her eyes. "Rah, rah, sis boom bah," she said dryly. But her eyes were twinkling behind their black eyeliner.

"Come on." Simone tugged on my arm. "We'd better get over there before Vinnie thinks we deserted."

As we headed for our teammates, my eyes searched for Logan. My heart gave a little jump as I spotted him. He was on the far side of the group doing bounce-kick drills with Matt and Darius.

All three guys were laughing, and Logan looked so happy and adorable I could hardly stand it.

"There he is," I told Simone. "Maybe I should go over and—"

"Aha!" A familiar voice rang out right behind us. "We were wondering when you'd show your face, Bailey."

Startled, I spun around. Megan and Ling were standing side by side with their cheerleading pom-poms at their feet. However, neither of them looked particularly cheery at the moment. Ling's arms were crossed over her chest, and Megan's hands were on her hips. Both of them were glaring at me.

"Hey, guys. What's going on?" I said uncertainly.

"We know what you did yesterday." Ling's voice was cold. "How could you go out with Logan behind my back?"

"Behind *both* our backs." Megan sounded more hurt than angry. "You knew we were going to tell him how we feel today!"

Simone frowned at them. "How did you guys find out about that?" she blurted out. Then she caught herself and shot me an apologetic look. "Oops, I mean . . ."

"So you knew about this?" Ling glared at Simone briefly before turning those piercing brown eyes back on me. "I guess it's true, then. I didn't want to believe it when my brother told me he saw you guys on campus yesterday."

"I *still* can't believe it," Megan put in. "I never thought you were sneaky like that, Bailey."

I frowned. After all her antics this past week, *she* was calling *me* sneaky?

Simone stepped forward. "Lay off, you guys," she snapped. "Bailey didn't do anything wrong."

"Oh, really?" Ling's eyebrows shot up so far they almost disappeared into her hairline. "So stealing someone else's guy isn't wrong? Interesting."

"He's not *your* guy," Simone retorted.

"Shut up, all of you," Megan said urgently. "He's coming!" She shot me a look. "We can discuss this later."

A second later, Logan and the other two guys jogged up to us. "Ready to kick some college butt, ladies?" Matt asked, stepping over to give Simone a quick hello kiss.

Meanwhile Logan was smiling at me. "Hey, Bailey," he said. "I thought about bringing Patch to watch the game, but I figured if a squirrel ran by, it'd be a disaster."

I forced a laugh, even though I wasn't feeling very cheery. "I think Vinnie's starting a huddle," I said. "We'd better get over there."

Usually playing in the Co-Ed/Lo-Ed games was a blast. But it was hard to enjoy myself under the circumstances. I had to admit it—I'd grown kind of accustomed to my popularity-adjacent status over the years. Once my annoyance wore off, I started to realize that all of that might be over.

That wasn't even the worst part, though. The worst part was remembering the hurt look in Megan's eyes. The disbelieving sense of betrayal in Ling's. Even though I'd been hanging out with them for years, I'd always thought of them as Simone's friends. Now, just a little too late, I realized that somewhere along the way they'd become *my* friends, too. Okay, so we didn't have much in common. That didn't matter—I still cared about them. Why hadn't I thought about that before? Maybe if I had, I would have talked to them about my feelings for Logan instead of assuming they wouldn't listen. Things couldn't have ended up any worse, right?

By the time the Lo-Ed team took the field for the third inning, I was feeling pretty low. We had more fielders than we needed, so Vinnie was rotating us on and off the field. This time I ended up at second base, while Zoe played first and Simone was out in right field. Logan was shortstop—a little too close for comfort. I was pretty sure he was trying to catch my eye a couple of times, but I was careful to face the pitcher's mound so I could pretend not to notice.

I also pretended not to notice Megan and Ling, who were cheering us on from the sidelines. Or at least that's what they were supposed to be doing. Mostly it seemed like they were standing off apart from Taylor and the other volunteer cheerleaders, just the two of them, talking with their heads close together. And occasionally staring at me. Great. Just one more thing to distract me from the game.

The first couple of Co-Ed kickers didn't do much, which made it even harder to pay attention. As I checked on Ling and Megan out of the corner of my eye, my mind kept rerunning the confrontation with them. It was really bad luck that Ling's older brother had spotted me with Logan, though now that I was thinking logically, I knew it had been crazy to think they wouldn't find out somehow. It was a small town, and gossip always traveled fast. I was a little surprised I hadn't noticed Ling's brother, but then again, I'd been too caught up in Logan to notice much of anything else.

"Heads up, Myers!" someone hollered.

I snapped out of my daze just in time to see that Susannah's boyfriend, Chuck, had just kicked the ball right toward me. Rushing forward, I scooped it up and whipped it over to Zoe, who tagged Chuck out at first.

"Good hustle, people!" Vinnie shouted from the pitcher's mound. "Keep it up!"

"Nice play, Bailey!" Logan called.

I chanced a look over at him. He gave me a thumbs-up and I smiled back weakly, flooded with memories from the day before. Being with Logan had felt so right, so fun and easy. Then there was that moment when I'd thought—no, *hoped*—that he might kiss me. . . .

I banished that particular memory as soon as it popped into my head. If I wanted to salvage my friendships, I had to stop thinking about stuff like that. I needed to make things right with Ling and Megan. Even if that meant backing off and letting them have Logan.

By the end of the game, which we lost by three points, I was determined to get it over with. Barely aware of Susannah and her teammates leaping and shouting in celebration all around me, I hurried over to the sidelines. Before I got there, Megan and Ling came forward to meet me.

"We've been talking, and we just want to know—why'd you do it?" Megan peered into my face.

I turned away, not quite brave enough to face their accusations head-on. "I don't know," I said impatiently. "I guess I thought—never mind. It doesn't matter now."

"Yes, it does," Ling insisted. "Seriously, Bailey. You've never even gone out with anyone before, right?"

"I know, I know, I'm pathetic." I sighed. "I guess I just went delusional for a while. But listen, I don't want to fight about this, okay? I'm sorry I went behind your backs, and I promise I won't do it again. He's all yours."

"What?" Ling sounded surprised. "Wait, Bailey. We're just trying to figure out what happened here."

"You already know what happened. I thought Logan was cute, I did something stupid, the end. But I'm really sorry, and I don't want you guys to hate me, so I'm backing off. I mean it. Okay?"

They just stared at me, not saying anything. I felt a flash of irritation. What more did they want? Did they expect me to swear an oath in blood before they'd forgive me? Or—my heart constricted as I thought of it—maybe they just *weren't* going to forgive me. The thought made me feel panicky and trapped, like a butterfly stuck in a specimen jar.

Finally Megan spoke. "Look, we're not telling you what to do," she said. "We're just asking what's up. I mean, you've been spending so much time tutoring Logan and everything, it's really not surprising if you started to have feelings for him."

"Can we stop talking about this, please? I already said you can have him!" I cried, so desperate to make them understand that my voice came out a little louder than I'd intended. "I'm telling you, I don't like Logan that way! I'm only spending so much time tutoring him because it will look good on my college applications."

Ling and Megan didn't answer. In fact, they were both staring at something over my left shoulder. Uh-oh . . .

I spun around. Logan was standing there. Had he heard what I'd just said? The answer was written all over his face. He looked shocked, angry . . . hurt?

"Logan, I—" I began.

Too late. He'd already turned and hurried away.

Chapter ☕ Twenty

stared after Logan, my heart sinking. I'd really blown it this time. And hurt a really cool guy in the process. Maybe the coolest guy I'd ever met.

But what was I supposed to do? I couldn't risk my friendships for a guy—I wasn't that kind of girl. Maybe now that I'd humiliated myself in front of Logan, Ling and Megan would forgive my temporary insanity. Maybe they'd even apologize for being such jerks to me. That was all I really needed—right? Then things could go back to how they were before. I could go back to my life plan.

"Bailey," Megan exclaimed. "Go!"

"What?" I said, turning toward her. Was she really going to be that way? To my surprise, she was smiling.

"Seriously, go." She reached out and gave me a little shove. "Go after him before he gets away!"

"What?" Ling and I said in unison.

Megan glanced at Ling. "You know we have to back off," she said. "Isn't that what we just spent the entire game talking about?"

Ling frowned. "I thought we hadn't decided for sure."

"Come on." Megan rolled her eyes. "It's obvious that Bailey's really into him. I can't believe we didn't see it before."

Ling glanced at me, not saying anything. Just then Simone jogged over. "What's going on?" she asked.

"Ling and I just realized Bailey really likes Logan," Megan said.

Simone snorted. "Well, duh. Took you long enough to catch on."

"I know, right?" Megan smiled at me. She didn't look upset at all anymore. "Now we just have to convince Ling."

"Fine, whatever." Ling wasn't exactly smiling, but she didn't look mad, either. "I'm convinced, okay? I wasn't really that into him anyway."

"Awesome!" Simone grabbed her and hugged her. Ling pushed her away, pretending to be annoyed. But this time she actually *was* smiling.

"So?" Megan gazed at me. "What are you waiting for?"

What *was* I waiting for? I could see Logan over by the dugout with some of the other guys. Even after what had just happened, I still felt that little flutter of sparks when I looked at him.

But was sparks enough? What was that, really? Just an

involuntary physiological reaction, a potent mix of adrenaline, dopamine, and probably a bunch of other brain chemicals I'd learn more about in med school someday. If that was all there was to it, I could get the same basic effect by skydiving or something. If that was all there was to it, maybe this thing with Logan wasn't worth all the angst and distraction. Maybe it was better to let him go. To stick to my plan.

Then I thought about the stuff my mom had told me the day before, about how plans don't always work out the way you think they will. How one little detail, like studying abroad, can change everything.

Could that first flutter of sparks have changed *me*? If it had stopped there, probably not. But those feelings had kept going, getting even stronger as I'd gotten to know Logan better.

And suddenly, just like that, I got it. There *was* something about him—something special. Something about *us*, Logan and me, together. Even Megan and Ling seemed to get it now. Looking at the evidence—especially that moment yesterday, when I'd been pretty sure he was thinking about kissing me—it was pretty clear that Logan felt it too. That he'd felt it all along. Or at least he had until . . .

I swallowed hard, picturing the hurt look in his eyes when he'd overheard me just now. Had I ruined everything?

"Well?" Simone sounded impatient. "Why are you still standing here with us when you could be over there smooching on your guy?"

I bit my lip, glancing again at Logan. His back was to me, so I couldn't see his face. Was it my imagination that his shoulders looked tense and angry?

"He might not want to see me right now," I told Simone.

With help from Megan and Ling, I filled her in on what had just happened. She winced when she heard what I'd said. But when I finished, she just shrugged.

"It doesn't matter. He'll forgive you." She sounded so certain, it was hard not to believe her.

"Yeah, just apologize." Megan smiled hopefully. "What have you got to lose?"

Ling nodded. "You've got to at least give it a try," she said. "Otherwise you'll hate yourself for wimping out."

She was right. They all were. Maybe I wasn't very experienced at this whole girl-boy thing. So what? Like my mom had said earlier, I'd never backed off from going after something I wanted before. If I started doing that, I'd never make it through med school. Or even high school, most likely.

I felt a flutter of nerves. Or was that sparks?

"Okay, here goes nothing," I muttered.

"That's the spirit!" Simone cried. She hugged me, while Ling and Megan patted me on the back.

Unfortunately, by the time I turned away from my friends, Logan wasn't by the dugout anymore. I hurried over to Matt and Darius, who were hanging out by the cooler of drinks Vinnie had brought.

"Where'd Logan go?" I asked them.

Matt chugged his sports drink. "Not sure," he said, his lips and tongue now bright blue. "He just took off."

"He went that way, I think." Darius pointed. "Said something about heading home."

"Thanks." I wandered off, feeling discouraged. So much for that. No matter how much I wanted to fix things, I wasn't going to follow Logan home. That just seemed a little too stalkerish to me.

A flash of color caught my eye, and I looked up. For a second I wasn't sure what I was seeing. It looked like a large purple bird darting and wheeling high up in the sky.

Then I blinked as it came into focus. It wasn't a bird—it was a kite. I realized the south end of Campus Lawn lay beyond the trees that edged the playing fields. I also realized that that was the direction Darius had pointed. . . .

Following a hunch—yes, scientists have them!—I headed that way. By the time I reached the tree line, I could see that there were several kites soaring over the green. My heart pounded as I stepped out of the trees, squinting in the midday sunlight.

I saw him right away. Logan was standing by himself a few yards ahead. His back was to me, and his head was tilted upward. Watching the kites.

Taking a deep breath, I stepped closer. "Logan?"

He spun around, looking startled. "Bailey?" He looked happy for a second. Then his face closed in on itself. "Oh. What do you want?"

When I saw the look in his eyes, I wanted to cry. But that wouldn't fix anything.

"I'm sorry," I blurted out before I could lose my nerve. "I know you heard what I said back there, but I swear I didn't mean it."

He looked wary. "Then why'd you say it?"

"Because I'm an idiot?" I tried. But no, that wasn't quite right. "Um, I mean because I thought Ling and Megan were mad at me. See, they've been having this stupid competition over you ever since you moved here, and then they found out I was hanging out with you outside of school, and they freaked out, and I thought . . ."

I trailed off, noticing that he looked completely confused by now. "Wait," he said. "What do you mean, they were competing over me?"

"They thought you were cute, I guess." I shrugged. "They're both sort of boy crazy, and they're also pretty competitive, so it just got a little out of hand."

That didn't seem to clear things up too much, at least judging by his expression. "Okay," he said slowly. "But I don't really care what they think of me. You . . ." He hesitated. "I don't know. You're different. I've never met anyone like you before."

My breath caught in my throat. "Really?"

"Yeah." He rocked back on his heels. "I don't know what it is. There's just something about you."

"I didn't mean that stuff," I said. The words all came out in a rush. "About only tutoring you to get into college. I like tutoring you—I'd do it even if I never got credit."

"Really?" It was his turn to look uncertain.

"I swear." I took a step closer. "I've never met anyone like you, either."

He stepped closer too. "It's weird, right? I've lived all over the place. Met all kinds of people." He hesitated, his eyes meeting mine. "Anyway, I'm glad my family's going to be staying this time."

We were less than arm's length apart now. I held my breath. He glanced up at the kites.

Then he took another step, and leaned toward me. I was pretty sure I was supposed to close my eyes now, but I didn't. What could I say? I was a scientist. I wanted to observe this.

His lips found mine. The sparks were all over the place now. I leaned into him, and felt his hand reach up and rest on my side.

I'm not sure which of us pulled away from the kiss first. But when we parted, we were both smiling. "Wow," he said.

"Yeah," I replied. "I know what you mean."

He leaned in for another kiss. This time I let my eyes drift shut, glad that I'd decided to follow my heart instead of my head.

At least just this once.

TURN THE PAGE FOR MORE FLIRTY FUN.

ourteen-fifty was a notable year for not only Europe, but for world history. Gutenberg's printing press is considered to be one of the most important inventions ever. If it weren't for that, you wouldn't have these books sitting on your desks." Mrs. Gregory paused. "Now, make sure to write all of this down, folks—there *will* be a quiz on it next week." She swiped her chalk-dusted hand across the black pants on her slim upper thigh and continued scrawling important dates about historical European events across the chalkboard.

I cast a sideways glance at Olivia, who shook her head and rolled her eyes. We were both thinking the same thing. Mrs. Gregory always threatened us with quizzes, but inside that tall, superthin body was a woman with a heart of melted butter. She went easier on us than most of our other teachers did, letting us pair up to study before tests and such.

Still, I took notes. Couldn't take a chance on looking like a slacker right now, not with everything riding on the line.

My big chance.

My stomach flipped and I shoved that thought aside. *Focus*. Surely we'd find out soon enough who got assigned to what positions in the sophomore class's end-of-year Renaissance faire. It was supposed to be today, from all the rumors I'd heard earlier at lunch.

"Mrs. Gregory," Karen said from her seat in the front of the class, thrusting her arm straight into the air. Her hair cascaded like a bright-red waterfall down her back, perfectly flat-ironed and one of my great envies. *Sigh*. What I'd give to not have boring brown hair. "When are we going to find out our parts for the faire? Isn't that supposed to be today?"

Apparently I wasn't the only one distracted during class.

Mrs. Gregory made a big show of glancing up at the clock over the doorway. She pursed her pale-pink lips and tapped her chin. "Hmm. I'm supposed to wait another twenty minutes to release you to the theater. The results will be posted on the double doors." She paused. "But if you're willing to work hard, maybe we can bend that a bit and I'll let class go a few minutes early."

My heart rate picked up to double time, and I nodded as the rest of the class buzzed in excitement around me. The response was unsurprising—most school activities were a little on the lame side, but the sophomore Renaissance faire was the highlight of the end of the year for the whole school, including the upperclassmen.

Even our teachers enjoyed it. Especially the way it brought out the students' competitive sides and made us work together to raise the most money we could for our school. It was tradition for the students to try to trump the year before, and our class was no exception.

As Mrs. Gregory turned back to the board to write faster, mumbling other important Renaissance dates out loud and scrawling key phrases beside them, Olivia slipped me a note. I unfolded it as quietly as I could—Olivia liked to twist and crunch them into the smallest pieces of paper possible—and read quickly.

Are you totally nervous?

"Nervous" wasn't quite the right word to describe my emotions. More like terrifyingly excited. Since waking up this morning, the results of the end-of-faire play auditions were all I could think about. I'd picked my way through breakfast and lunch, trudged from class to class as each minute painfully clicked by.

I just hope I got a good part, I wrote back, crumpling it in a ball and tossing it in her lap. Luckily, Mrs. Gregory didn't really care if we passed notes, so long as we kept it subtle and it didn't distract anyone else. I wouldn't dare try it in another class.

Our teacher talked on and on, continuing to alternate between writing and patting the back of her low bun. I wrote notes without listening while stealing peeks at the people around me. A few were goofing around—mostly guys whispering and elbowing each other. One girl, Liana, was completely asleep in the back, her face buried in the crook of her arm on her desk. Nothing new there—I doubt she'd been awake for the majority of the year. Then my attention caught on Jason Hardy's shrewd brown eyes where he sat in a desk two rows to my left.

He raised one eyebrow at me.

I tore my gaze away, a hot flush crawling up my cheeks. Jason—the bane of my existence. A big pile of arrogance mixed with just enough cuteness to let him get away with treating people like dirt.

Olivia tossed me another note. *He's soooo cute.* Obviously, she'd seen me giving Jason the hairy eye.

Only if you like them tall, dark, and totally obnoxious. I tossed it back to her.

She read it and pursed her lips, shooting me The Look. The one she'd given me since last year that indicated she thought I was judging him too harshly. Frankly, due to what we'd both heard about him, plus my own personal run-in with His Royal Majesty, I felt like I wasn't judging him harshly enough.

Still, I shoved aside my irritation and turned my attention back to my sparse notes. Jason didn't matter right now. I had bigger fish to fry, and I knew that because Olivia had an unrequited crush on him, it was a sensitive area in our friendship. One I'd been careful to respect by avoiding the topic whenever possible.

Mrs. Gregory stepped away from the board and moved to the front of her desk, jumping up to sit on the corner. "Okay, notebooks away. Hurry it up," she added, urgently waving her hands at us. She gave a minute for people to get packed up and finish talking then continued. "As you know, the sophomore Renaissance faire is one of the shining highlights of our school year. We get news coverage from a local station, and even a reporter from the paper comes by. The entire sophomore class participates in this *mandatory* function, including decorating the gym. No one job is more important than anyone else's. All the teachers have consulted with each other and worked together to assign your positions."

A few of the guys in the back groaned, but most of us were engaged and quiet, waiting to hear more.

"Mrs. Gregory," Timothy said from two seats behind me in his slow, easy country drawl—he'd moved to Cleveland in elementary school from Georgia but still hadn't shaken the accent. "What if we don't like what we're assigned to do?"

She gave him a small smile. "Learn to like it." Turning her attention back to the class, she swept her gaze over all of us. "You are being graded on full participation, enthusiasm, and creativity for both days of the faire. You must bring your historical and literary knowledge into your projects or assignments. We expect you to do your best. And, of course, helping the school fund-raise is an added bonus."

I fought the urge to squirm in my seat. Playing it cool was key right now. *Fake it till you make it* was something my mom always said. The decision had already been made, and soon enough I'd be finding out if my audition merited a role in the pinnacle of the faire—our student play.

"Okay, then." Mrs. Gregory gave a big smile and stood. "You're all dismissed. Go straight to the theater to find out your assigned roles. And don't try to skip out," she added loudly above the sudden noise of twenty-five students scrambling for the door. "I'm going there too and will be watching you."

I grabbed my books and tucked them into the crook of my arm. My heart was pounding so hard I could barely think straight. It was silly, getting so nervous about a play. And yet, this could be my chance.

Olivia squeezed my hand, a huge smile on her face. "I'm so excited for you! Let's go!" She practically dragged me into the hallway, her blond curls bouncing with each step. There were clumps of sophomores streaming by us. Apparently other teachers had the same idea as Mrs. Gregory.

The theater felt a thousand miles away, and it didn't help that when we arrived, the place was far too packed for us to reach the doors. Rows upon rows of students were clustered tightly together, and nearly all of them were taller than my barely five-foot height. No way could I get through this crowd or see overtop of it. *The pains of being short,* I thought with a sigh.

"I can't see a thing," I said to Olivia, standing on tiptoes in the futile effort of eyeing the door.

"I have an idea. Stay here." Olivia slipped between two people in front of me and disappeared.

The noise got louder as people talked over each other in excitement, with a few frustrated groans popping in and out of conversations. I overheard snippets, smothering more than a laugh or two behind my hand.

"—wanted to wear a pretty gown, but I have to dress like a serf—"

"Your armor is going to look awesome! Wait until—"

"—*hate* the recorder . . . I haven't played it since fourth grade."

"Abbey!" a voice called out, ringing overtop of everyone else in Olivia's typical commanding fashion. "Oh my God!" Then I saw her push back through the crowd toward me, a huge smile splitting her face. Her brown eyes shone in excitement. "Oh my God," she breathed, "you got it! *You got it!*"

"What did I get?" I asked, trying to speak past the sudden lump in my throat. "Am I in the play?"

Olivia grabbed my arm and dragged me a few feet away from the crowd. "Okay." Her grin grew crooked. "First off, I saw that I'm in charge of the puppet show. How funny is that?" She shook her head. "I barely know how to work a puppet, much less write a show, then make the full cast and create a set. Still, at least it's more fun than peddling turkey legs—sorry, *legges*—to the crowds."

"I'll be happy to help you with the puppet stuff," I replied, giving her a big smile. "It'll be great."

"But that's not the coolest part." She paused, gripping my hand. "You got the lead, Abbey. You're the female star of the play.

In addition to now helping me with the puppets, of course," she added with a wink.

A big squeal bubbled out of me before I could stop it. "Oh, wow!" I reached over to hug her. "This is the best day ever!" In my gut I'd felt my audition was good enough to warrant me a speaking part . . . but never could I have dreamed I'd get the lead. That was reserved for the upper clique, people like Karen, who achieved every accolade possible in school.

The play was a Renaissance-era romantic comedy, pitting two brothers against each other as they tried to win the hand of their childhood friend Rosalyn.

My character. The lead female.

The realization was overwhelming, thrilling, and I squeezed Olivia harder.

Olivia pulled back, her smile wobbling a little. She put her hands on my shoulders, glancing down then flicking her gaze back up to me.

"What's wrong?" I asked.

"Um, there's one other thing. I think it's great news, but you might not be so thrilled." She swallowed. "Don't shoot the messenger, okay?"

Somehow I knew what she was going to tell me; something in my gut had a nasty feeling. Still, I had to hear it from her to confirm. "What is it?"

"Well . . . Jason Hardy got the part of the male lead."

Leave it to him to ruin the happiest moment of my entire

sophomore year. I heaved a large sigh, the wind sapped from my sails.

Olivia dropped her arms, her face going flat in an instant. "Come on, now. Don't be like that."

"I don't want to get into this right now," I said as quietly as I could. Which was hard, considering the surge of irritation boiling in me. "Let's get out of here."

We made our way to our lockers then met at the back door of the school a few minutes later. The early May air was balmy and warm, a refreshing change from being trapped in our stale school and the typical Cleveland-area rainy spring. Buds erupted and blossomed into bold-colored flowers on the green-leafed trees lining our path to my house. Birds chirped and danced along the sidewalk, bouncing on tiny feet and pecking at spots on the ground.

A gorgeous afternoon . . . but it wasn't enough to make me feel better.

I shouldered my bag higher.

"I can tell you're not happy," Olivia said, her footsteps in perfect rhythm with mine—an old habit we'd started in middle school when walking back and forth every day. "But you should be. Even if you don't like Jason, this will force you to give him a chance and see him in a new light."

"But I don't want to." I crossed the street, knowing I sounded petulant but unable to resist adding, "And actually, I *did* give him the benefit of the doubt before—this is where it got me."

"I can't believe you're still upset over that. It was last year." Olivia sighed. "He's different. Yes, I know he was a jerk before, but he's not like that anymore." Her voice took a soft edge that drilled back into my head about how big her crush was growing.

It was that crush that kept me from spouting off about all the ways Jason was awful. The many, many, *many* ways. Instead, I bit my tongue, for the sake of my best friend, and we made our way back to my house.

Why am I letting him steal my moment? That sudden thought jarred me. I straightened my spine as I keyed the lock to my house. Jason might put a damper on this moment, but I deserved to celebrate my success. I wasn't going to let him take that from me.

"We need ice cream," I declared, heading right into the kitchen as she dumped her bag on our living room sofa. "To celebrate the start of a successful Renaissance faire."

I was determined to make this the best play, the best *faire*, the school had ever seen.